I0640137

FURTHER BEYOND

A LOVECRAFTIAN SCIENCE FICTION NOVEL

FURTHER BEYOND

A LOVECRAFTIAN SCIENCE FICTION NOVEL

BRIAN STABLEFORD

WILDSIDE PRESS

Copyright © 2017 by Brian Stableford.
All rights reserved.

Published by Wildside Press LLC.
www.wildsidebooks.com

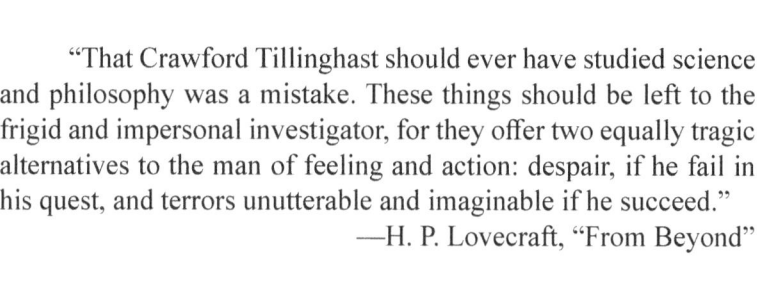

"That Crawford Tillinghast should ever have studied science and philosophy was a mistake. These things should be left to the frigid and impersonal investigator, for they offer two equally tragic alternatives to the man of feeling and action: despair, if he fail in his quest, and terrors unutterable and imaginable if he succeed."

—H. P. Lovecraft, "From Beyond"

I

I had known, of course, that Crawford Tillinghast had correspondents—one might almost say colleagues—with whom he discussed his work in progress, for science is not, like sorcery, the work of isolated and secretive individuals working from the pages of soiled grimoires. It is the work of men who know that they are engaged in a collective endeavor directed toward understanding, who know that clear and far sight is only available to those who stand on the shoulders of giants. Scientists seek useful information from men working in adjacent fields, and are ever willing to discuss and debate what they glimpse, by mail if not in person.

Even so, I was surprised when Tillinghast's former correspondents began to contact me, in the immediate aftermath of the scientist's tragic demise, with an evident urgency. Three, in particular, seemed galvanized by his sudden death, and were extremely eager to know whether I had removed any notes, diagrams or calculations from his house on the night of the disaster, or where such documents might be located if I had not. They were eager, too, to obtain a more complete account of my experience on that occasion than the broadly truthful but rather minimal account that I had been prepared to give to the police.

The police had arrested me as soon as I recovered consciousness, simply because they had found me in a room with a dead man, holding a gun in my hand that had just been fired. They took me to the central police station in Providence and kept me in a holding cell while they pursued their enquiries at the scene—although they did, in all fairness, send a doctor to attend to me there, to make sure that I had not sustained any injury in the explosion.

By the time that the detective in charge of the case finally got around to questioning me, however, he had ascertained that the only shot fired had hit and apparently smashed Tillinghast's machine, and that the scientist had died of apoplexy. He had no reason to doubt the account that I gave him, and seemed rather relieved that it dovetailed so well with the facts he had ascertained, permitting him to file a coherent report. I told him that the machine—whose function, as a non-scientist, I could not begin to understand—had apparently gone awry during the demonstration that my friend had invited me to witness and had begun releasing some kind of strange ultraviolet radiation, which had caused both of us to experience hallucinations. Not knowing how to switch it off, and in the grip of panic and vertigo, I had fired at it, before passing out. Tillinghast had apparently not been so fortunate.

Having concluded that Tillinghast's death was due to natural causes, the focus of the police investigation had shifted to Tillinghast's servants, who were missing. I told the lieutenant, honestly, that I had no idea what had happened to them, but hypothesized, quite reasonably, that if the hallucinatory radiation had affected them too, even in a milder fashion, they might well have been induced to run away.

At the time, the lieutenant had accepted that hypothesis meekly as the most likely one. A case of missing servants, even if there are three, is inherently much less important than the possible murder of a man of Tillinghast's status—his wealth, that is, rather than his reputation as a scientist. It was only two days later, when it had proved impossible to find any trace of the supposed runaways, that the lieutenant questioned me again, very briefly and discreetly, after Tillinghast's funeral, although I was unable to give him any further information.

It was after the funeral, too, that I heard from concerned neighbors of Tillinghast that muted malicious rumors had begun to circulate that the "mad scientist" might have murdered the servants. So far as I know, however, the police did not change my poor friend's official status from that of suspected murder victim to suspected murderer.

I saw Rachel at the funeral, of course, and gave her my sincerest condolences, but funerals are such formal affairs, and so crowded—people flock to attend the funeral rites even of relatively reclusive men, especially if they are well off—that I did not have an opportunity to speak to her in private. She promised to contact me in a day or two in order that we could do so in easier circumstances. I was introduced to James Patterway at the funeral too, but for similar reasons, he contented himself with saying that he would contact me again the next day in the hope of arranging a more convenient meeting. I responded vaguely, making no promises.

The rumors concerning Tillinghast's suggested madness also involved me, and one or two people actually attempted to make enquiries of me, in order to reassure themselves. Apparently, the doctor who had been commissioned to examine me in the holding cell at the police station, viewing me at the time, incorrectly, as a murder suspect, had doubted my statements about the radiation of the machine and its hallucinogenic effects. Casting around—quite unnecessarily—for alternative hypotheses, he had apparently made the bizarre suggestion in his report that I had been hypnotized by Tillinghast, and that what I seen, or thought I had seen, was due to his suggestion.

The doctor had also mentioned in the report that I had "confessed" that I had been suffering from certain optical anomalies, which I knew from experience to be preliminary to a migraine. Again quite unnecessarily, he had noted that I was prone such migraines, and often used laudanum to treat them. I had mentioned those facts casually, as matters of no importance, but the doctor, his imagination inflated by his official status and involvement in what he thought at the time to be a sensational murder, had pounced on their melodramatic possibilities. In the wilder rumors, therefore, I was being cast as a drug-addicted sorcerer's apprentice prone to delusions. My friend's interment and its aftermath would have been a deeply upsetting occasion in any case, but the glances and whispers of the hangers-on made it even less bearable.

I had not told the police about the evident deterioration in Tillighast's mental state that had taken place in the ten weeks before his death, but other people obviously had, lending abundant fuel to the circulating rumors. I cannot tell what effect they might have had on the policemen involved with the attempt to locate Tillinghast's butler, Gregory, his housekeeper, Mrs. Updike, and his cook—whom I only knew by the name of Jane—but I dare say that they too had a certain professional temptation to favor melodramatic hypotheses over the humdrum, and the questions they asked of all and sundry would only have added fuel to the fire.

I had not said anything to the police, either, about Tillinghast's metaphysical theories regarding other worlds existing in parallel with our own, unapprehended by our limited senses, even though that was, strictly speaking, highly relevant to the case. In the two days following the funeral I was extremely glad about that omission, because it was easy enough to guess how that would have added to the suspicion that he was a "mad scientist" and perhaps given rise to pleasantries in very poor taste regarding the disappearance of the servants.

Had I mentioned Tilinghast's remarks, on that last day, regarding his ambition to weaken or break down the barriers separating our material system from those hypothetical other worlds, it might even have give rise to reportage in the yellow press, the time of year being reputed in press parlance as "the silly season." It was bad enough that I was receiving insistent communications from Tillinghast's correspondents; I certainly did not want sleazy reporters banging on my door.

Fortunately, Tillinghast did not seem to have mentioned to any of his neighbors his conviction that he had already found a means of stimulating the sensory—or perhaps extrasensory—powers of the pineal gland, in order to allow him to catch glimpses of those other worlds coexistent with ours and their terrible inhabitants. The three correspondents to whom he had confided that conviction were scholars, who would never have dreamed of talking to newspaper reporters, so the discomfiting rumors remained local and subdued, bound to peter out eventually and be forgotten, as such rumors usually are.

I had, of course, told the police that what I had seen was purely a matter of hallucination, because that is what I sincerely believed. I did not doubt it at the time, and even when I did begin to doubt it, in consequence of the events that I am about to relate, I refused to abandon that hypothesis entirely. Looking back, I can see clearly that it was what I desperately wanted to believe, and I had very good reasons for that desire, and its desperation. Even now, when I certainly cannot believe *sincerely* that it was all a matter of delusion, I am glad of the mental recourse of telling myself that it might have been, because the alternative is too horrible. I can cope easily enough with the notion that there might be unspeakable horrors elsewhere in the vast universe, but not the thought that I might be one of them.

* * * *

Knowing my limitations, Tillinghast had, of course, only given me the sketchiest account of what his machine was supposed to do, but he had obviously given fuller accounts to some of the people with whom he made contact, in the hope that their knowledge and expertise might supplement his in the further pursuit of his enquiries. In a sense, they knew far more about his endeavors than I did, especially because one of the petty quarrels that occasionally disturbed my long and close friendship with him had distanced me from him in the crucial ten weeks before his death. On the other hand, none of them—even Patterway—had ever actually met him in the flesh, whereas I had known him since childhood, had been in his company during the last few hours of his life, and had actually experienced the effects of the bizarre mechanism he had invented. That meant, in the view of Tillinghast's confidants, that I undoubtedly had knowledge that might usefully supplement theirs in their attempts to pick up the threads of his endeavor and carry it forward. Given that, their eagerness to see me, albeit a trifle belated, was understandable.

Tillinghast's former correspondents were not the only ones who got in touch with me in the aftermath of his death, so it was a busy and difficult time, and I had good excuses for not responding to their urgings as promptly as they probably would have wished. Nor, in fact, was I the only person they had approached with a similar belated urgency and ardent desire to obtain a privileged share of his secrets. When Rachel wrote to me the day after the funeral, fulfilling the promise given to me then and expressing her desire to arrange a meeting in the near future, she mentioned that she had already heard from the three philosophical vultures circling the corpse of his ambition—although she did not, of course, express it in those terms, that image being my own.

The image of the three as metaphorical vultures was, I suppose born as much from my unsympathetic attitude to Tillinghast's scientific endeavors and the fragile state of mind in which his fatal experiment had left me as from the insensitivity and avidity of their behavior. Although the poor opinion I formed of them in advance of meeting them was not entirely unwarranted, I ought to admit that it was partly due to prejudice on my part, and was not entirely just either. No matter how hard I tried to believe that everything I had seen in the presence of the diabolical machine was mere hallucination, I could not deny that the experience had shaken me badly. Although I was certainly not the opium-addled nervous wreck that some of the crueler rumors seemed to be painting me. I was definitely not myself in the days following Tillinghast's death, and I was well aware of it. I am willing to admit, therefore, to a certain oversensitivity in respect of the three scholars who wanted to interview me about my friend's ideas and the events leading up to his death. That sensitivity was further augmented by the knowledge that they were also pestering Rachel.

It was not only in respect of my attitude to the vultures, of course, that the oversensitivity in question was manifest. I had one bad migraine on the eve of the funeral, and another the day after. On both occasions I tried to resist taking laudanum, having long been warned about the dangers of over-frequent use, but on both occasions I eventually gave in. Furthermore, I was convinced that the ordeal would continue, and that more migraines would follow—a nagging anxiety that probably increased their likelihood, almost acquiring the status of a self-fulfilling prophecy. In addition to that, I continually found myself looking round nervously, and even looking behind me and *looking up*, afraid of what I might see. I had no clear idea of what I was afraid of seeing, but I had no doubt that it was sinister, horrible and predatory.

I continually assured myself that it was "all in my mind" and that it was "just a phase I was going through," but there are times in life when clichés ring hollow, partly because they are mere clichés, referring to the normal run of events, and thus woefully and pathetically inappropriate to circumstances outside that normal run. Such was my state of mind in the aftermath of Tillinghast's death that normality itself seemed somehow to have slipped out of my reach, in need of recovery.

I say my "state of mind" because I was careful, at that time, not to say "state of being." I did not want to consider, let alone admit, that the experience the machine's radiation had forced me to undergo might have wrought a permanent change in me. I did not even want to imagine the possibility that the radiation in question, rather than administering a momentary and transient stimulation to the pineal body in my brain, had somehow triggered a slow but definitive alteration of its anatomy and its sensory capacity. What I desperately wanted to believe was that what I had experienced on that fateful night was no more than the immediate and fleeting product of my own frightened imagination, suggestively stimulated by Tillinghast's fragile mental condition: something that could not endure.

If Tillinghast had not been my best friend, and I had not been his, I suppose that I might have been prepared to entertain, or even eagerly to grasp, the doctor's suggestion that I had been hypnotized, and that the hallucinations had been of his contrivance. It was, however, too utterly absurd to think that a friend of his caliber, even if he had been driven mad by obsessive scientific fascination and relentless labor, could ever have wanted to play such a puerile trick on anyone, let alone me. Tillinghast was a serious man; he did not stoop to trickery only worthy of stage magicians, Mesmerist charlatans and a few honest alienists. As for the notion that anything I experienced thereafter might have been due to some kind of post-hypnotic suggestion, I would describe that as unthinkable if it were not for the fact that I have just written it down, and therefore have at least thought of the necessity of eliminating it from consideration.

I also wanted to believe, albeit not desperately, that Gregory, Mrs. Updike and Jane really had simply run away, frightened by what they had seen in the house in the weeks before Tillinghast's death, and by their master's deteriorating state of mind. He had told me in so many words that they had been "disintegrated," but I did not think that I needed to take that assertion at face value. I thought it perfectly plausible that it was a delusion on his part—indeed, that it was good evidence of his delusional state and proof that his other allegations regarding the inhabitants of other dimensions were merely a reflection of his fears, not reasonable extrapolations of his strange hypotheses.

At any rate, I certainly did not want to believe that the three missing individuals had been murdered, either by human hands or by horrid creatures from some subtle world parallel to our own, hidden from us by the intrinsic limitation of our senses. I wanted to believe, or at least to hope, that they were still alive and happy, if not in our world then in another, perhaps having undergone some benign metamorphosis. If I were to entertain the notion of metamorphosis at all, I thought at the time, I dearly wanted to think of such processes as benign. Tillinghast had, after all, been quite insistent in the course of his final mad tirade that his "pets" had not *hurt* his servants, and although his supplementary remark that disintegration was painless undermined the reassurance of that remark, the invitation was still there to think that, even if his more extravagant hypotheses were true, Gregory, Mrs. Updike and Jane were unharmed.

* * * *

The "vultures" who had taken the trouble to make insistent en-quires of poor Rachel as well as me were, as I have said, three in num-ber. I have already mentioned Patterway; the names of the other two were Crisson and Dove.

James Patterway was a Professor of Natural Sciences at Miska-tonic University. Miskatonic is notorious in academic circles—and far beyond, including the yellow press—for its possession of a collection of manuscripts and strange artifacts brought back by various pioneer-ing expeditions financed by its wealthy benefactors, to such far-flung regions as the Gobi desert, the jungles of Yucatan and Antarctica. Many of the University's staff, in various disciplines, have taken an interest in those documents, some of which are said to be unique, and have attempted to investigate their alleged contents—I say alleged because their translation has posed enormous difficulties and given rise to nu-merous controversies—in various ways.

Unlike the majority of his colleagues, who regarded the decipher-able parts of the documents as accounts of legends, of interest only to anthropologists and historians of religion, Patterway had been prepared to take seriously the possibility that they referred to actual entities, which had made their presence felt in the material world in the remote past and, although seemingly long-dormant, might still be capable of exercising such a presence in the right circumstances.

Tillinghast had contacted Patterway in order to consult him re-garding the possibility that the entities in question might belong to the parallel worlds in which he was interested—and what, if that were the case, his machine might be expected to discover in offering at least a window to one or more of those parallel dimensions, and perhaps a means of building viable bridges of some kind between the worlds. A considerable correspondence had developed from that contact, although it was soon interrupted, and its very brevity had evidently whetted the biologist's appetite to know more.

Robert Crisson was, like Tillinghast, an amateur scientist inclined to favor unorthodox ideas simply because they were unorthodox and decried by the defensive conservatism of "official science." He was the scion of a family enriched in the distant past by the slave trade, to a far greater extent than Tillinghast's coal-owning family, and in the nearer past by shrewd capitalist dabbling, who had elected to devoted himself to a passion for electrical science. He must have been initially inspired by the example of Thomas Edison, the renowned Wizard of Menlo Park, and apparently still hoped to become an inventor of note, but his attention had been deflected away from mere mechanical tinkering toward more fundamental issues of the physics and metaphysics of electricity, taking more inspiration from Edison's great competitor Nikola Tesla, and perhaps also from the great English pioneers of electrical science, Michael Faraday and Andrew Crosse.

Tillinghast had consulted Crisson about the technical possibilities of his machine, seemingly intent on picking his brains, but the two men appeared to have retained a certain guarded suspicion of one another, natural to scientists afraid that the fruits of their genius might be stolen and put to profit by others. They had been in the process of slowly cultivating a mutual trust that would have allowed them to stop exchanging vague generalities and teasing hints when the correspondence had been rudely interrupted, doubtless leaving Crisson with a considerable degree of frustration. He appeared convinced that he might have been on the brink of learning something immensely useful to his understanding, and perhaps profitable in terms of practical applications, and that he only required a few more hints to enable him to make a crucial breakthrough.

Lyman Dove was…well, I have to confess that I never did find out at the time exactly what Dove considered himself to be, and I never settled subsequently on a succinct label. I gathered in the course of our exchanges of ideas that he would not accept the label "psychic researcher," or that of "parapsychologist," any more than he would ever have condescended to describe himself as a spiritualist or a Theosophist. I formed the vague impression that he might have been a failed literary man before interesting himself in the mysteries of the plenum, as so many lifestyle fantasists are, but such evidence as he provided was suggestive and indirect, and I soon learned not to expect overmuch clarity from him.

Nevertheless, Tillinghast undoubtedly knew Dove to be a widely-read man, and apparently thought him ideally qualified to supplement Patterway's somewhat overspecialized knowledge of the Miskatonic arcana with a generalized overview of the legacy of research into various uncanny phenomena carried out under the auspices of the British and American Psychical Research Societies, the Theosophists, and the "harmonic societies" that thrived in France in the first half of the last century. He had presumably been as coy in communicating the practical details of his research to Dove as to Patterway and Crisson, with the same effect of whetting an appetite of curiosity left conspicuously unsated by his untimely death.

My immediate response to the enquiries of the vultures had been very negative, not merely in the trivial sense of flatly denying that I had any of Tillinghast's papers in my possession but also in the more assertive sense of telling them that I had no wish to meet any of them, or even to write them an account of what I had experienced, or anything else. I stopped short of telling them to go to hell in so many words, although I was tempted.

Rachel's letter requesting a meeting was a very different matter, because it answered a long-contained ardor of my own. She was Crawford Tillinghast's widow—his "relict," as legal jargon sometimes puts it—but she had once been far more to me than that, and had continued to be, albeit in a carefully veiled fashion, after her change of status.

Tillinghast had been my closest friend for as long as I could remember, and our friendship had very deep and sturdy roots; it could not have been sustained otherwise, given that we had drifted apart intellectually to such an extent that we no longer had much in common in our ideas and interests by the time he died. We had known one another as little children, however, when we had been inseparable, and it had seemed both natural and inevitable to maintain our friendship at college in spite of the divergence of our academic interests. Even then, our fellow students thought Tillinghast eccentric and ill-tempered, and felt slightly uneasy in his company, but I knew him far better than they did, and had long since learned to weather the occasional storms of his personality. That is perhaps a learning process only possible for children, because adults find temper tantrums far more discomfiting, but once the habit is formed, it holds true. Perhaps he was a trifle eccentric, even a little odd, in addition to his problems of self-control, but he was also brilliant, handsome, charming, devoid of social conceit and steadfastly loyal—in a many ways, an ideal friend.

It had been Tillinghast who met Rachel first, because she was a laboratory technician at the college where he and I were students, but she was the same age as us and lived not far from the apartment we shared. Initially, when Tilinghast introduced me to her, it was merely as a casual social acquaintance, hardly even a friend, and it was in that context that the three of us initially met up together, with increasing frequency, although each of us occasionally saw her on our own as the bonds became firmer. I was on the very brink of confessing to Tillinghast that I had fallen in love with her, and that I intended to propose marriage to her without further delay, when he anticipated me and made precisely the same confession to me.

Perhaps, if I had spoken first, his loyalty to me would have persuaded him to shelve his own ambitions and keep silent, as I did in the event, but that is a matter for pure conjecture. Why did I take that course of action? I have often asked myself—and needless to say, have often regretted it. I have often thought, belatedly, that perhaps I should have been honest and matched his confession with mine, but I did not. That was not because I was afraid that he might become angry with me, or that he might claim priority on the grounds of having met her before I had, but because I was direly afraid of what might happen if we both put our confessions to Rachel and asked her to choose.

Quite simply, I could not believe, at that time, that Rachel could possibly have chosen me over him. Tillinghast seemed to have all the advantages, in terms of looks, wealth, genius, and even passion—a passion unusual, and perhaps even disadvantageous, in a man of science. I thought myself exceedingly drab by comparison, not without reason, and I therefore suspected that if Rachel were forced to make such a choice overtly, it might ruin my relationship not merely with her but with Tillinghast, making it impossible for me to continue being friends with either of them. Better, I thought then, to accept the defeat gracefully and not admit to a temerity that would probably have been unwarranted. I did not know, of course, how persistent my love would be, or how painful it would become.

As time went by, I not only became increasingly critical of my cowardice, but increasingly doubtful of the accuracy of my judgment—and, for that matter, theirs. I began to wonder, albeit without any real basis for the suspicion, whether there might not have been a possibility that Rachel would have chosen me, had I only thrown my hat into the ring. More importantly, I became increasingly convinced that she had made an error of judgment in marrying Tillinghast, who, in spite of all his good qualities, did not have what was necessary to make her happy. She had not known him as a child, she had not adapted psychologically to his occasional outbursts of ill temper, and she was a very sensitive person.

Prior to the marriage, Rachel had only seen those outbursts second hand, as it were, directed at me, and had perhaps assumed that they were confined to our particular relationship. When she became their occasional object, they hurt her deeply—and because of that, they began to hurt Tillinghast deeply too. He regretted them terribly, and must have made heroic efforts to contain them, but could not always succeed, and the cumulative effect they had on Rachel was agonizing for me to observe, all the more so because no soothing intervention on my part seemed possible, on either side. Tillinghast was never physically violent, with me or with her, but that unbreakable restraint only seemed to increase their internal intensity.

In between those brief fits, they were very loving, and seemingly very happy, but the gradual wear and tear inflicted on the relationship by the rare outbursts nevertheless had an insidious and cumulative effect. When the two of them eventually made the decision that it would be better to live apart henceforth, all three of us were heartbroken, and I am ashamed to admit that my share of that heartbreak only had a tiny component of sympathy for them, the bulk of it being anguished remorse for a wasted opportunity to make a marriage that would have not only been the happiness of my life but might conceivably have allowed both of them to remain happier than they seemed to have been condemned by circumstance to be.

When Tillinghast and Rachel separated, in the seventh year of their marriage, casual acquaintances readily made the suggestion that it was because his love of science was greater than his love for her, and that she had been wounded by neglect as well as intimidated by his periodic outbursts of wrath, but I can declare with the utmost confidence that that was not the case. It was simply that Tillinghast found it far easier to *express* his love of science than his equally passionate love for Rachel, at least in the conventional ways expected—demanded—by New England society. It was not the depth of his passion that was at fault but its mask, and it was not neglect that wounded his wife but an intensity of feeling that seemed to her to be too awkwardly formulated, even when it was expressed very differently than in his explosions of frustration, to be easily bearable. In the event, they lived apart for one year more than they had lived together, but neither of them ever sued for divorce, or, so far as I know, sought solace in any other intimate relationship.

After the marriage, of course, I continued to have a relationship of sorts with Rachel. She was my best friend's wife, and I always made every effort to be her friend too. She certainly seemed to consider me as a good friend, and our friendship was not without warmth, although neither of us would ever have dreamed of overstepping the limits of propriety. It always seemed to me, however, that the bond between Tillinghast and Rachel was somehow located on the opposite side of his personality to the bond that linked him to me. Ours was a linear rather than a triangular community, and Tillinghast loomed so large between myself and Rachel that she seemed over time almost to become invisible to me: a significant presence in my life as well as his, while they were together, but always in shadow.

I think, too, that from Tillinghast's viewpoint the bonds that linked him to Rachel and me, although very different in kind, were almost equal in strength. I believe that the trust that Tillinghast had in me was as indissoluble as his love for Rachel, even if it did not arise from the passionate element of his character. I believe that he was utterly convinced that he could always depend on me, even though others thought me cold and indifferent to everything, and in spite of the fact that his excitability sometimes led him to quarrel with me and banish me temporarily from this presence. At any rate, I always tried to live up to that trust, and my exile rarely lasted more than a matter of days, or a few weeks at the most.

In spite of the warmth of the friendship that I had with Rachel, therefore, we were distanced by the nature of Tilllinghast's different relationships with the two of us. While they were living together I felt, over time, even though I saw her fairly frequently, that I began to lose contact with Rachel's present self, even though the person that I had met, admired and loved remained bright in my memory, and was still cherished very dearly, in spite of the fact that the memory of my love remained locked away, as a possibility that had been eclipsed by circumstance.

It occurred to me, of course, that I might renew closer contact with Rachel after her separation from Tillinghast, and might even try to reformulate the potential for a different relationship. The prospect was tempting, but the project seemed impossible, firstly because of the formal reason that she was still legally married to Tillinghast, and secondly because, in spite of the separation, I knew full well that Tillinghast still loved her, in his own way, and that any move on my part to court his wife would have seemed as much of a betrayal as if I had tried to seduce her when they were living under the same roof. As I say, I believed that I had a responsibility to Tillinghast's expectations of me that I could not violate.

When I met Rachel at the funeral, I had not seen her for several years. We had run into one another several times after the separation—the society of Providence and the surrounding region is a small world, and its geography is a trifle narrow—but we had both been very guarded in our questions and comments, each equally careful of failing in our duty to Tillinghast. We had not been able to be comfortable any longer in one another's company.

Now that Tillinghast was dead, however, the spectrum of possibilities seemed to have shifted markedly, although there were still awkward matters of decency and propriety standing in the way of any change of policy on my part. In addition, perhaps encouraged by the unease of my state of mind, I felt uneasy about my own feelings, and how those feelings might develop if they were freed from their long captivity, impelled after an interval of fifteen years to seek what had once seemed to be a highly desirable culmination. I could not measure the exact extent to which time had changed me, and had no idea how it might have altered her, so I hardly dared try to guess whether any renascent hopes flickering within me at the thought of seeing her again might me be mere illusions, doomed to gutter and become extinct in the cold light of present reality.

Even if I had not been nurturing long-buried feelings, however, I could not possibly have hesitated over my response to an appeal from her. Whatever she wanted of me she had a right to ask, and I had a duty to provide. But how, precisely? What was the most appropriate way of reestablishing contact? As she had written to me in a formal manner, I thought that propriety demanded that my initial reply ought to be in writing. I immediately wrote in reply to her letter to say that I was completely at her disposal, that she was very welcome to visit my home in the suburbs of Providence, or that I would be equally glad to visit her in the coastal village where she had taken up residence, not far from New Bedford, at a moment's notice.

She wrote again, with equal immediacy, to thank me, and to assure me that she would take full advantage of my kindness. As the sole heir to Tillinghast's estate, she told me, she would need to spend a few days—perhaps at much a week—in his house, of which she was now the owner, in order to take a personal inventory of its contents, to decide what was to be done with both the movable and immovable property, and also to complete the legal formalities regarding the execution of the will, involving obligatory visits to the bank and the town hall as well as the lawyer's office. She asked me to come and see her there on the evening following her arrival, and, if possible, to remain on hand long enough to lend her what assistance I could in her sad task.

I could not refuse, of course, no matter how intimidated I was by the prospect of returning to the scene of the tragedy: a house that I could hardly consider as anything but haunted, having seen what I had seen there and suffered the trauma that I had suffered. But the machine had been destroyed, and I was fully entitled to hope—or so I thought at the time—that all its effects had been destroyed with it. And even if they had not, what kind of a coward would I have been if I had left Rachel to face any residual effects alone?

Because time was short, and the communicative ice had been broken, I took the liberty of telephoning Rachel in order to agree to her proposal. She thanked me earnestly, and I realized that she might have been intimidated himself by the thought of going to the house alone. How much she knew about Tillinghast's experiments and theories I had no idea, but even if he had told her nothing, the enquiries she had received from the vultures, on top of the disappearance of the servants and mutterings about her husband's alleged insanity, might well have alarmed her. At the very least, she had to consider that there was a mystery about the house and what had happened there, and one of the reasons for her request that I meet her there—perhaps the principal reason—was obviously the hope that I might be able to help dispel that mystery and dissipate any possible sensation of menace.

"There's a small hotel where the by-road that leads to Tillinghast's house joins the highway," I told her. "It's less than a mile away. I'll reserve a room there."

"Pease don't, David," she said. "To be honest, I'd much rather have you stay in the house, at least for the first night and perhaps longer. I'll bring Stephen, my chauffeur, with me, as well my maid-of-all-work Emily, so we won't have to fend for ourselves, and I really don't think that our being under the same roof will give rise to any gossip...not that I care if it does. Besides which, you might well have difficulty booking a room at the hotel. It's very small, and *they*'ll be there."

"Who?" I asked, a trifle stupidly.

"The unholy trinity: Patterway, Crisson and Dove. They're all exceedingly keen to acquire the wreckage of Crawford's machine, and all his other equipment—not to mention his papers. Only Crisson has so far put in a cash bid, but Patterway is insistent that everything ought to go to Miskatonic, in order that it might be properly preserved and evaluated. I suspect that I might be able to stage an interesting auction—or perhaps start a small private war—if I assemble them all in the same room, along with the wreckage of the machine and any papers I can find in the house. Before I let any of them in, though, I feel that I need some moral and intellectual support—support that only you, in all probability, could effectively provide. Will you be my knight in shining armor, David, to defend my confusion and poor Crawford's honor against the scholarly marauders?"

What could I say, except that I would be delighted? And in a way, I was. For her to describe me as her "knight in shining armor" was of course, only a colorfully flippant manner of speaking, but it was a role that I certainly thought that I could relish, even if the old flames that I had once imagined to be flickering within our relationship turned out to be utterly dead and incapable of being rekindled.

On the other hand, I couldn't help feeling that, from another angle—albeit one that I was trying hard not to take up—answering Rachel's appeal might lead to dire inconvenience and discomforts. Not only would I have to confront that damnable haunted house again, but I would apparently have to do so in the presence of avid carrion-birds, who would be intrusively curious at best, and perhaps ominously suggestive regarding the implications of Tillinghast's theories and actions. I was not at all surprised that Rachel felt that she needed a protector to ward them off—but I was not sure that I would not need one myself, and was direly afraid that my knightly sword might turn out, when tested, to be made of cardboard.

However, there is a code of behavior imposed on anyone summoned to play the role of knight, which sternly forbids any refusal to enter the lists, even against dragons, giants and ogres. There is no specific mention of migraines in Medieval romance, but plenty of vaguer references to illness, to hallucinatory visions of all sorts and to monsters; knights are supposed to suffer such things bravely, and conquer them—or die trying.

"I shall be delighted to serve as your loyal knight, my lady," I assured her, hoping that I did not sound as if I were making too light of the matter, or too much. Delighted I was, but also grimly determined, and perhaps secretly convinced, without wanting to admit it to myself, that a defense might indeed be necessary, against enemies even more redoubtable than three unorthodox but thoroughly civilized scholars.

2

I was very well aware of the time required to complete a journey between my home and Tillinghast's, because I had made the journey so frequently, so it was not a careless miscalculation that led me to arrive more than two hours before the time suggested for the meeting, and thirty minutes ahead of the estimate that Rachel had given me of the time of her own arrival. Given that I had to go, and to go in the capacity of a lady's champion, I wanted to check the place out in advance—or, rather, I wanted to check myself out, in proximity to the house, to make sure that I could tolerate the environment. For that reason, I took care to reach the house while the sun had not yet begun to turn crimson as it sank slowly toward the wilderness of the west, but was still blazing benignly yellow in a clear blue sky.

I did not take a motorized cab from the tramway terminus, having always felt more comfortable in horse-drawn transport, but I regretted that slightly, for the final section of the road that led to Tillinghast's isolated house was even more replete with ruts and potholes than I re-membered it, and I felt certain that I would not have been jolted nearly as much by a vehicle with pneumatic tires as I was in the two-wheeled trap. Many a time in the past, I had ridden out the jolts with casual dis-dain, but now, I was frightened that they might start my head aching, with the henceforth-inevitable accompaniment of spots before my eyes. The driver, too, seemed direly resentful of the road's condition—for which he naturally blamed me personally—and he set off on the return journey sulkily, with a pained expression on his face, as if fearful that his frail vehicle might disintegrate under the stress.

I carried my bags to the front porch and set them down beneath it, outside the door. Then I began a circumnavigation of the house. I could have gone inside immediately—I knew where Tillinghast had hidden his spare key, and I was sure that no one would have removed it, even if the police had found it while searching the premises—but it did not seem polite to anticipate Rachel in that respect, and I was confident that I could make an initial assessment of my own state of mind as easily by looking in through the windows as by going inside.

I ambled around the house and its annexes. I sniffed the air, very different from that of the city, in which the odors of the sea were perceptible, even though the location was a full mile inland, albeit on a hill from which the ocean was distantly visible. Those odors should have been perfectly familiar, but there seemed to be an odd quality about them, which might have been an effect of the time of year, marine vegetation reaching a point of maturity and decline at the end of August just as terrestrial vegetation does, but might also have been purely psychological.

Nor was it simply the country air that seemed to add to my unease. The house, too, should have seemed abundantly familiar, Tillinghast having lived there for nearly fifteen years, during which time I had visited him almost to a monthly basis, often staying overnight and sometimes for several days, but the night of the scientist's death seemed to have drawn a firm line under that phase of my existence, and the sensation of developed familiarity had been suddenly banished. In the warm afternoon sunlight, the house seemed peaceful, and would undoubtedly have appeared at least quaint, and perhaps charming, to an unbiased observer, but to me, in the aftermath of my trauma, it seemed alien, and haunted. To be more specific, it seemed to be haunted, in some strange fashion, from *above*, as if something were weighing upon it, balanced for the moment, as if on the spike of its weather-vane, which doubled as a lightning-conductor, but with a precarious equilibrium that might break at any moment.

I told myself, obviously, that it was all in my mind, and commanded myself to put such puerile ideas out of my head, but the fact remained that as I circled the house, slowly and painstakingly, I felt that I was circumscribing a region of danger, a region tainted, perhaps forever, by the arcane quest that Crawford Tillinghast had undertaken there, in his capacity as a modern alchemist.

As I went, I peered cautiously through the windows, which seemed to have attracted an unusual amount of grime since they had last been washed. I tested the kitchen door, which gave access to a small vegetable-garden, to make sure that it was properly locked. I sat down briefly in the part of back garden devoted to flowers, where there were also half a dozen apple trees. Gazing at the flowers and the trees, with my back to the house, reassured me that everything was natural and placid, that there was no cause for unease—but as soon as I stood up again to resume my circumnavigation, that reassurance dissolved, and I had to resume instructing myself not to be silly, and to get a grip on myself.

I looked up, once or twice, at the windows on the first floor, and the smaller ones in the mansard roof that concealed Tillinghast's laboratory, but for some unaccountable reason, I stopped the direction of my gaze there, reluctant to contemplate the ridge of the roof or the weather-vane—and I kept my hat on while I did so, so that the slightest adjustment of my head would bring its protective brim into play, like a shield.

I checked out the shed where the electricity generator was housed, and saw, somewhat to my relief, that it was inactive. It would mean that Rachel and I would have to rely on the old oil lamps and wax candles for lighting once darkness fell, but, perhaps oddly, that thought did not bother me in the least. Electric light banishes shadows far more effectively than lamplight, but the idea of electric current flowing invisibly around me somehow seemed, for the moment, more ominous than shadows. I did not know why, but it seemed to me that the unspecifiable threat lay more in brightness than in darkness.

I did not see anything authentically untoward in or around the house in the calm afternoon light, beneath a sky whose scattered clouds were reassuringly fleecy. I could hear the weather-vane, though; there was an unsteady breeze blowing, sometimes from the east and sometimes from the south-east, from the not-so-distant sea. The metallic vane—whose ornament, I knew from memory, was shaped like a fish rather than the conventional cockerel—creaked as it swayed, obedient to the atmospheric indecision.

I knew that the sound of the weather-vane was perfectly natural, but it seemed to there was something else up there, perhaps beyond hearing as well as beyond sight, that did not seem quite *right*. Yet again I told myself sternly that the sensation was purely subjective, a product of my own obstinate anxiety, but I could not help remembering that Tillinghast's machine had somehow retained a visible glow even when it appeared to me that its electricity supply was switched off—that the buoyant entities revealed by that glow had seemed to carry it with them when they moved into the surrounding walls, and up into the roof.

Tillinghast had claimed that the glow was ultra-violet light somehow made visible, but I could not see that the assertion made any sense, and I had suspected even at the time that the interpretation was a symptom of mental derangement—but however nonsensical his suggested identification might have been, and whatever else might have been illusory, the glow itself had certainly been real. The surroundings of the machine had been affected by its experimental use; the radiation had indeed permeated the attic floor and the mansard roof.

Perhaps, I thought, as I continued my stroll, the entire house had been affected by it, in a subtle but nevertheless substantial way—and perhaps the weather-vane had been affected most of all, given its metal constitution and the fact that the machine must have been positioned directly underneath it, in close proximity to it. Then I told myself yet again not to be silly, insisting that it was all in my mind, trying to tell myself that that even the glow of the machine might have been mostly in my mind, which had transformed a perfectly innocuous light into the first symptom of a hallucination.

* * * *

When I got back to the front of the house again, after twelve or fifteen minutes, perhaps a little more confident in my sanity by then, there was a man standing just outside the porch, looking down pensively at the luggage I had left beneath it. There was no horse or vehicle outside the gate; he must have arrived on foot, although I did not remember passing any pedestrians as I was following my own jolting course along the road.

We looked one another up and down. He was tall and bony, perhaps forty years of age, with a tanned, leathery complexion and eyes as dark as his near-black hair. He was dressed respectably and unostentatiously, in a gray suit, with a dark blue cravat and sturdy shoes; he was holding a fedora in his left hand and a stout cane in his right. My own homburg was in my right hand by then, but I hadn't removed it out of politeness; I had begun fidgeting with the brim while on the prowl after leaving the section of the garden where the apple trees were.

He had the advantage of me. Of the three vultures who had contacted me, the only one I had met in the flesh was Patterway, and I knew that this was not him. Given that he was staying in the same hotel as his two rivals, he presumably knew that I was neither of them, and that allowed him to jump to the correct conclusion.

"Mr. Dearden, I presume," he said.

I almost hazarded a guess when he paused, but he saved me the trouble. "Lyman Dove," he supplied. "I wrote to you, if you recall." He transferred his cane to the hand in which he was holding his hat in order to offer the right to be shaken. I accepted it, reluctantly, but let go as soon as I could without being offensive.

"I recall," I said, curtly. "Mrs. Tillinghast isn't here yet—didn't she give you an appointment?"

"Oh yes," she said, "but I wanted I take a look at the place in advance—to soak up a little of the atmosphere, as it were. Mrs. Tillinghast mentioned that you would be here at eight, but I didn't know that you would be coming in advance as well. I apologize if I've inconvenienced you in any way."

I did not accept the apology—nor did I offer him one, although I suspected that my presence might be inconveniencing him more than his was inconveniencing me.

"The breeze is always welcome at this time of year," I observed, although I knew perfectly well that the "atmosphere" in which he was interested was no mere matter of molecules of air. "Cooling, without bringing the odor of fish from the coastal canneries."

"Do you still find that odor noticeable nowadays?" he asked. "Since the cod began to shun the cape that bears their name, I rarely catch a whiff of that industry. I'm almost nostalgic for it, on occasion—although I ought to be grateful for anything that helps to keep my sensory channels clear. There is something odd in the air, though, don't you think?"

"No," I lied. "You're presumably unacquainted with the quality of Rhode Island air at this time of year."

"True," he admitted. I've spent most of my time in New York and Boston since returning from Europe. Even so…I have the oddest sensation that the odors blowing from the sea on the breeze are being supplemented by something descending from above."

"It's all in your mind," I assured him.

"Isn't everything?" he countered, amiable. "Not that I'm a solipsist, mind. You knew Dr. Tillinghast well, I understand?"

"Very well," I said. "We grew up together, as close as brothers. Our lives diverged, as lives inevitably do, but our friendship remained unshakable."

I said that proudly, and it was only afterwards that I wondered whether it had been wise to insist, given that it was bound to give him the impression that I knew more about Tillinghast's work and his fatal machine than I actually did."

"And you were with him at the end," he continued.

This time, I contented myself with a simple "Yes."

I half-expected him to follow up with the accusatory observation that I had destroyed the machine, but he did not.

"I hope that experience has not had too traumatic an effect," he said. "It must have taken an effort of courage for you to come back here." I wondered whether he had seen me before I had seen him, and whether he had had the opportunity to observe my unease, the facial evidence which, assuming myself to be alone, I had not made any effort to conceal.

"Not too traumatic," I assured him.

"But it must have had a deleterious effect on your migraines."

I was literally shocked by that remark—not simply by the fact that he had somehow obtained information about my medical condition, but that he was rude enough to bring the matter up in conversation when we had only just met. I knew that there had to be some kind of hidden agenda in the statement, some kind of exploratory probe, but I did not consider that his curiosity licensed such impertinence. My immediate temptation was to reply "What migraines?"—but to do so would have seemed like an admission of weakness, conceding some kind of advantage to him.

I did not immediately jump to the conclusion that Dove had been actively investigating me, although I had been alerted to the fact that a private detective had been asking questions, presumably having been hired to discover whether I had any of Tillinghast's papers. When I had heard that, it had seemed to me that the man most likely to have hired such an agent was Robert Crisson, who had the money that allowed him to indulge in such frivolous luxuries. It seemed more likely that Dove was taking a guess based on something else he knew—or thought he knew.

Two can play at that game, I thought.

"My migraines are under control," I informed him, lying again. "How are yours?"

"Too controlled, alas," he replied, serenely. "Consciousness is such a traitor, at times, is it not? We think of it as the vehicle of the will, but that is too narrow a view. Such will-power as we have is, for the most part, channeled through it, but its principal role is to function as a protective wall. James Patterway, of course, thinks that the wall was erected to filter experience wisely rather than simply to imprison us, but he's an exceptionally narrow-minded man. Do you know Patterway?"

"We've met," I confirmed. "I didn't find him narrow-minded at all. Quite radical in his thinking, in fact."

"I suppose he might be considered deeply eccentric if he were at Yale or Princeton, but there's a difference between being radical and being open-minded. At Miskatonic, in any case. he definitely qualifies as a conservative, if not actually stuffy. Indeed, it seems to me that he wears his narrow channels of thought as a badge of pride, mistaking them for scientific rigor and scrupulousness. Expectable in any university man, I suppose, although Miskatonic has more exceptions than most. Have you met Robert Crisson too?"

"No," I said, not wanting to stretch insincerity to the point of blatant irony by saying that I hadn't had the pleasure.

"He's more open-minded, as befits a dilettante condemned to unorthodoxy—but I fear that he has one of those minds in which openness sometimes tends to vacancy. He's the real adversary, of course, if the four of us are in competition—or rather, his money is. Patterway has his professorial status, though, and you have…the appeal of friendship, I suppose."

I took note of the fact that Dove seemed to be assuming that I was there for the same reason as everyone else: to try to take possession of Tillinghast's work, or part of it. At the very least, he was fishing in order to discover whether I really was a rival, or an accidental custodian of valuable information, or perhaps merely an inconvenient bystander. I didn't bother to correct his misapprehension—or rise to his bait, if he was merely attempting a ploy.

"And what do you have, Mr. Dove?" I asked.

"Only my charm," he said, smiling as if it were a joke. He must have read in my face, however, that I'd taken the remark the wrong way. "Oh, I've no intention of behaving toward Mrs. Tillinghast in any way unbefitting a gentleman. What I hope to do is to seduce all five of us into an amicable and fruitful collaboration. Crisson's not malicious or jealous by nature; it's only the possession of his money that tempts him to play the monopolist. He can be persuaded to be friendly, I hope. Patterway's more of an intellectual hoarder, but he's not unreasonable; he'll probably bend, if pressure is cleverly applied. How about you, Mr. Dearden? Are you a team player or a one man band?"

"That isn't the way I look at the situation, Mr. Dove," I said. "To be perfectly honest, I don't care about your fatuous competition to take possession of the debris of Crawford Tilinghast's work. Mrs. Tillinghast has just lost her husband, and I really don't think that she ought to be subjected to the kind of harassment that you, Patterway and Crisson seem intent in inflicting on her. I'd far rather that all of you showed a little decency and discretion."

"Not a team player, them" he said with a contrived sigh. "A pity—especially as you appear to have valuable evidence that I'm not the only one avid to solicit. In all fairness, though, I don't think that my requests for information have amounted to harassment. Mrs. Tillinghast had been separated from her husband for eight years. That's bound to have taken a little of edge off her grief, don't you think?"

"No," I said, bluntly, "I don't." I glanced down at my watch, Rachel was already late. I wondered whether there was any way of getting rid of the importunate Dove before she arrived.

"Well," he said, casually, "I bow you your superior judgment, as you've known her for such a long time—and in that case, I'm truly sorry if my urgency has offended or upset her. I hope she'll understand, however, the importance of the matters at stake. How much did she know about her husband's work, do you think?"

"Nothing at all," I told him, bluntly, "so there's no point in pestering her with questions. I know very little about it myself, and I suspect that if you, Patterway and Crisson pooled your information, you'd have an enormous advantage over us. Perhaps you'd be better off holding a colloquium at the hotel and forgetting about Mrs. Tillinghast altogether."

"I shall certainly attempt to arrange exactly such a colloquium," he said, "being a team player myself—but even if the three of us do pool our information honestly, there will be several key pieces missing from the jigsaw."

"The wreckage of the machine? It's quite useless, the explosion having shattered it into deformed smithereens. I don't know Mrs. Tillinghast's intentions as yet, but as it's her property, I think she would be perfectly entitled not to hand it over to you, or even to forbid you look at it, if she so wishes."

"Well, we shall have to hope that she isn't as curmudgeonly as you are, Mr. Dearden. I take your point about the effects of the explosion, and I wouldn't be able to make head nor tail of such a jigsaw, but Crisson seems to believe that all he requires is a glimpse of the machine or its plans to able able to duplicate Tillinghast's work."

"Even if Tillinghast did make detailed plans of the machine—and it wasn't his way, and he certainly never showed any to me—it would probably be very unwise to try to repeat his work. It ended very badly."

"Perhaps so—but it seems that you had something to do with that. In any case, scientific curiosity is a powerful force, not easily opposed, even by explosions, death and rumors of madness, sorcery and monsters."

"Monsters?" I couldn't help querying. "What monsters?"

"What monsters, indeed?" he countered, cheerfully. "Given that you seem to be the sole survivor of those who might have seen them, I was rather hoping that you might tell me. I have my suspicions, but as a scrupulous scholar, I await the evidence before formulating hypotheses."

"The rumors are all nonsense," I told him. "The radiation of the machine induced hallucinations, that's all."

"Perhaps so," he said, again. "But I, at least, would be very interested to know the nature of those hallucinations. If my suspicions are correct, I can understand your reluctance to talk about them, but believe me, Mr. Dearden, you won't find many ears as sympathetic as mine to your story."

I found his manner extremely irritating, although I knew that the unease caused by my tour of the house might have something to do with that.

"Well, for myself," I said, "I'm in no need of a sympathetic ear, and I don't care about the suspicions about which you're dropping such careful hints. I hope that Mrs. Tillinghast refuses to have anything to do with you."

"Well, for myself," he countered, "I'm glad to say, Mr, Dearden, that there's no longer any possibility of that. The fact that Mrs. Tillighast has invited the three of us to come here suggests that she's at least willing to talk to us, and to show us the debris of the machine. As for the pieces of the puzzle that you hold, are you really determined to keep those entirely to yourself?"

It was a good question. I felt that I was on the back foot, losing the argument.

"I've already told you that I don't possess any relevant documents," I said, stiffly, "and that I hadn't seen Tillinghast for several weeks before the day of his death, with the consequence that he didn't have a chance to keep me up to date with the progress of his experiments."

"But you were here on the evening of his death," Dove pointed out, scrupulously keeping any hint of hostility out of his voice. "You were the only witness to the operation of the machine and its effect… the only surviving witness, that is."

"You said that before," I remarked, "But I see no reason to suppose that Gregory, the cook and the housekeeper are dead. As I've told the police, I think they simply left because they were frightened."

"Which would have been plausible if they'd been found," Dove pointed out, with justification, "but time has passed, and there seems to be no trace of their movements after they left the house, if they did. I sincerely hope that my suspicions as to why that might be are unjustified, but every passing day increases my suspicion that I am not."

Yet again, he was dangling his "suspicions" before me like bait on a fishing line. I didn't like that, and it increased my stubbornness considerably.

"I refuse to believe that they're dead," I said.

"As is your right," he assured me, letting his sarcasm show, "but you must admit, Mr. Dearden, that your refusals do not constitute evidence."

As soon as the words were out of his mouth he seemed to regret having voiced them, and I got the impression from the curl of his lip that he was admonishing himself offending me, when the effect he wanted to achieve was the opposite. "But that's by the by," he was quick to add. "The point is that you and I ought not to quarrel, because we're to the same side. We both want to understand what happened when Dr. Tillinghast activated his machine, and we both have information that might be relevant to that understanding. You might not believe my assertion that I have useful insight, and you might be even less inclined to believe me when you've heard me out, but I really do think that it's in your interest to hear me out, and I can't see that you can possibly lose anything by it."

He was right, of course, and I regretted having somehow put myself in a position of entrenched hostility. Much as I disliked having to do it, I had to mount a tactical retreat, as gracefully as I could.

"Look, Mr. Dove," I said, "as you say, Mrs. Tillinghast has invited you, Patterway and Crisson here, presumably with the intention of satisfying your curiosity in some measure. In view of that, I'm willing to do likewise, in the hope of putting an end to what really does seem to me to be harassment. It also seems to me, however, that the least you can do in return is to respect the terms of the offer she's made you—which is to say, that you ought to wait until the time arranged for the meeting, when she and I can address the three of you together. Attempting to steal a march on your colleagues in his manner doesn't seem to me to be the act of a 'team player,' or a gentleman."

He laughed, apparently genuinely amused. "Well, perhaps not," he admitted. "But curiosity is a powerful force, as I say, and it wouldn't surprise me at all if one of the others—Crisson, probably—hasn't been here already to take a long look around. I'll certainly inform my…colleagues…of your entirely legitimate concerns. It's not my intention, or theirs, to upset or annoy anyone; we all have every interest in maintaining friendly relations with the people we think capable of aiding us in our personal quests. So, until later…."

He put his hat back on his head and turned away; but he was too late to make his exit in what I would have considered to be a timely fashion. Already twenty minutes later than the time she had indicated to me as the likely moment of her arrival, Rachel Tillinghast's Model T Ford was powering along the roadway, lurching from side to side as it hit the potholes.

I hoped that the vehicle's pneumatic tires and suspension-springs were cushioning Rachel and her maid from any substantial bruising.

3

Lyman Dove and I watched the automobile draw to a halt. I was quick off the mark in racing to open the rear door of the vehicle, to offer Rachel a greeting less effusive than I could have wished, swiveling my eyes to indicate Dove's inhibiting presence. I moved on swiftly to offer to help her with her luggage, but she assured me that the chauffeur did not need any help. She took the arm that I offered her and moved closer to me in order that we could confront the unwelcome visitor together, with a united front.

I left Dove to introduce himself, but he did not seem to notice the impoliteness, and bowed very gracefully after removing the fedora again. He did not apologize for his untimely intrusion, though.

I suspect that Rachel wanted to tell him to go away and come back at the agreed time, in a peremptory manner, but she seemed a trifle flustered by the situation as a whole, and employed a desire to give further instructions to the chauffeur, with regard shopping for supplies, as a pretext for turning away.

In order unlock the door, and then to answer her summons, the chauffeur had deposited the first set of bags under the porch alongside mine, and left them there. I went to pick them up and carry them inside, leaving Lyman Dove standing on his own, ignored. Unfortunately, with my hands full, I was unable to close the front door behind me, and Dove took advantage of the circumstance, impertinently. He was inside before anyone could devise a stratagem for keeping him out.

Rachel settled for continuing to ignore him. She concentrated all her attention on me when I came back downstairs again to collected the second set of bags, which the chauffeur had also ferried to the doorstep before turning in his heel in order to execute the commissions he had been given.

Rachel didn't tell me that I hadn't aged a bit since the last time she had seen me, perhaps because it would have been too evidently untrue. I might more plausibly have paid her the equivalent false compliment, but it didn't seem necessary. She hadn't put on much weight—remarkable in a woman who had been a trifle stout even in her twenties—and her angular face was still relatively wrinkle-free, but her hair had begun to go grey and she had not condescended to begin dyeing it. Her best feature was still her frank blue-green eyes.

She thanked me profusely for coming, and insisted a trifle too lavishly on her regret at not having seen me for so long and her gratitude to me for keeping my friendship with her husband so firm.

"When the police told me that you had been arrested, I was outraged," she said. "If you had fired a gun, I told them, it was certainly not at my husband. That was unthinkable. You might very well, I said, have been defending him—but attacking him, never."

"The error was of short duration," I assured her. "The lack of a bullet-hole in the body told that story for me—although it took a little longer for the Medical Examiner to determine the true cause of death."

"Crawford was always a victim of his unreliable capacity for passion," she said. "His explosive excitability was bound to expose any flaw in his make-up eventually—and the brain is such a delicate organ, so prone to sudden hemorrhages."

"He'd been working too hard, I fear," I told her. "Science benefits from commitment—one might almost say obsession—in a purely methodological sense, but there is often a human cost to be paid for such long hours and deep commitment. I'd often urged him to take more rest, and more exercise, but he felt that he was reaching a climax in his achievement, and couldn't be persuaded."

I had to be a trifle diplomatic; I didn't know whether she had seen his body before its cremation, and whether she knew the extent to which he had changed.

"I'm glad that you were with him at the end, David," she said.

I had no reply to that—certainly not "So am I"—and Dove, who was not even bothering to pretend that he was not eavesdropping on the conversation, could contain himself no longer.

"It's a great shame that your defense proved unavailing, Mr. Dearden" he remarked, belying his claim to natural charm, "and an even greater shame, from the viewpoint of science, that your bullet hit the machine." He didn't ask what I had actually been firing at, perhaps slyly hoping to prompt Rachel into asking the question, or one akin to it—but she didn't rise to his bait either.

"I believe we have an appointment for eight, Mr. Dove," she said, coldly. "In the meantime, David and I have private matters to discuss. I don't mean to be rude, but I must ask you to leave now, and come back at eight."

He had grace enough not to scowl at the summary dismissal, and merely said "Of course. Until eight, Mrs. Tillinghast, Mr. Dearden," before putting his hat back on again and leaving, weaving around the remaining luggage on the doorstep and making no attempt to close the door behind him.

Rachel sighed with relief.

"It could have been worse," I said. "You might have found all three camped on the doorstep."

"Let's start again," she said. "Honestly, David, I really am delighted to see you. It's been far too long. You and I used to be such good friends. Marrying Crawford ought to have maintained that, but somehow he…well, in a strange way, he seemed to come between us…and then the separation made things doubly awkward. It's my fault, I fear. I really should have made more effort to maintain contact with you."

"It wasn't your fault at all," I assured her. "The responsibility was entirely mine. I was the one who failed, if there was any failure."

"No, you didn't," she said. "You were showing your usual tact and delicacy. And now I'm taking unfair advantage of you, not only asking you to come back to a place that must surely evoke bad memories now, however many good ones remain from the old days, but asking you to help me defend myself against Mr. Dove and his insistent…are they his friends, or his adversaries? But to be honest, I simply couldn't bear the thought of coming back here on my own, let alone facing the Scientific Inquisition unaided. There really wasn't anyone else I could turn to."

"If there had been, "I said, "I certainly hope you would have selected me in any case, as a matter of preference. I'm only too glad to help, I assure you."

"There you go again," she said. "Always tact and delicacy. You're a marvel in your way, David, even by the exacting standards of New England."

I wasn't at all sure that Lyman Dove would have agreed with that judgment. In fact, I was certain that he wouldn't.

"Pick up your bags and bring them upstairs," Rachel added. "Put them in your old room."

Not "the guest room," I noticed, as Tillinghast would undoubtedly have called it, but "my old room," as if I were the only person who had ever stayed there during the early days of the marriage.

Rachel followed me upstairs and came into the guest room in order to cast a critical eye over it. "Not up to Mrs. Updike's usual standard," she observed. "Emily will give it a thorough dusting tomorrow, but I fear that she and Stephen will be rather busy this evening, restoring the ground floor to a measure of respectability. At least it's not damp."

"Its fine," I assured her. "I'll be perfectly comfortable. It's practically a home from home."

"Come down to the study," she said. "We'll be better able to talk there."

As we moved back to the main staircase she cast a glance at the second wooden stairway at the far end of the corridor, which led up to the attic laboratory, but she made no comment. Neither did I.

There were two leather armchairs in the study, a large leather-topped desk, a thick carpet, and impressive bookshelves lining the walls.

"The lawyer forwarded all the papers from the desk drawers and the laboratory, except for those he needed to complete the execution of the will, to New Bedford," she told me. "I've brought back all of those that seem to pertain to Crawford's work, although I suspect that I wouldn't be able to make heard or tail of them even if his handwriting weren't so nearly illegible. There's no detailed plan of any kind of machine, and the record of his experiments is exceedingly sketchy. There might well be more documents here, I suppose—not hidden, obviously, but carelessly stuffed in between the books. Will you help me search, David? Not now, obviously—perhaps tomorrow, while I'm in town taking care of the obligatory tedious paperwork."

"Of course," I said, "But you know what Crawford was like. A powerful mind and a scrupulous memory, but he wasn't one for scrupulous record-keeping. I doubt that there's anything to find."

"So do I," she agreed, a trifle distractedly, "but we ought to make sure."

Suddenly, she fixed her eyes upon me in a confidently imperious fashion: the gaze of a woman who knows perfectly well that she is staring at someone incapable of refusing her anything. "Tell me the truth about what happened on that last evening, David," she said, quietly. "The whole truth, not what you told the police. No tact and no delicacy, just for once. I really need to know."

It was a command. I obeyed, as I was obliged to do.

I told her everything—or almost everything.

I told her how surprised and disturbed I had been by the change in her husband's appearance and manner, although I did not go into excessive detail regarding the precise extent of that change, and how disturbing it had seemed at the time—and still seemed, in informed retrospect.

I gave her a brief synopsis of what her husband had said about beings possessed of different senses being able to see a very different world from the one perceived by ours, and the possibility that the space around us might contain entities normally invisible and intangible, but perceptible with aids more artful than such optical instruments as the telescope, the microscope and the spectroscope. I reported the conversation as if it had been calm and scrupulously scientific, without mentioning the peculiar intensity that Tillinghast had put into it.

In passing, I mentioned that the electric lights had been switched off, and that the house was only illuminated, after dark, by lanterns and candlelight—as it would have to be tonight—and that Tillinghast had told me that there was a definite reason for that, without explaining what it was. I told her that I had assumed at the time, and still assumed, that it was in order to make the strange light surrounding the machine more clearly visible. I really had assumed that at the time, and was still prepared to assume it, although I now had some marginal doubts.

"So the generator was still working, and the supply to the house was functioning?" she queried. "It was only the electric lights that were switched off."

"Yes, although the machine seemed to be powered entirely by acid batteries rather than being connected to the generator. It wasn't actually running when we first went up, though. Tillinghast definitely seemed to switch the machine on, although I couldn't see the switch from where I was sitting."

I told her then what Tillinghast had said about "dormant organs" and the pineal gland, again making it sound like a scrupulously scientific discourse. After that, I moved on to describe the sensations that had overtaken me as the radiation of the machine began to affect my brain: the sensation of unreality, replaced by that of being in a void, and the strange impressions of sound and an air current.

"Such sensations weren't entirely unfamiliar," I told her. "They reminded me in some ways of effects I've observed when taking laudanum for my headaches. They seem to be not untypical of the drug's effects—Thomas De Quincey describes similar ones in *Confessions of an English Opium-Eater*—so they didn't seem to me to be entirely alien. In fact, initially, I thought I was simply coming down with a migraine, because the visual phenomena that often precede a migraine are not dissimilar to the ones the machine provoked."

"You still have trouble with migraines, then?"

In the old days, I had tried to conceal that vulnerability, but I couldn't conceal it from Tillinghast, nor, after the marriage from Rachel.

"Yes," I admitted, but I didn't tell her that they had increased in frequency of late. In spite of her prohibition, I couldn't avoid tact and delicacy entirely. I glossed over Tillinghast's reference to finding Mrs. Updike's clothes in a heap after she had unwisely switched in the electric light downstairs, and the hypothesis that she had been snatched away by creatures from "a hideous world." At the time, I hadn't believed it, and I still didn't, although that doubt, like many others, had increased.

I did, however, describe the kaleidoscopic sensations associated with the seeming dissolution of the solid structure of the house, the numinous things that seemed to drift though that compromised solidity, including those that seemed inky and gelatinous, stressing Tillinghast's firm assertion that they were harmless and repeating my own assertion that they were similar to the temporary delusions induced by my migraines.

"There's a simple medical explanation for those," I assured her, "and given that, it seems only rational to assume that what I saw in the attic was a more intense version of the same phenomenon: a product of the brain. Crawford, however, didn't suffer from migraines and probably hadn't ever used laudanum. Even if he had, its effects aren't consistent, so he might not have drawn the same analogies. His immediate assumption had to be that what he was seeing was real, and he reacted accordingly. I think that's why he died. It got to the point where I couldn't stand it any more, in spite of knowing that it was all mere hallucination, and if I'd reached that degree of panic, I can't imagine what he was feeling…."

I was getting ahead of myself, though, and tried to put that judgment into context. I reproduced some of Tillinghast's rhetoric regarding the illusory nature of time and matter, and his conviction that the stimulation of his pineal gland had allowed him see "beyond the bounds of infinity." I admitted his conviction that "things that devour and dissolve," coming from further afield than the world of illusion that I could see for the moment, were "hunting him" as they had allegedly hunted the servants, but I stressed that he was in a state of feverish excitement and that he was undoubtedly suffering from delusions.

"But if you knew that it was all delusory," Rachel said, quietly, "why did you fire that gunshot—and what were you firing at?"

"There comes a point when knowing that you're suffering from induced delusions isn't enough," I told her. "The delusions are still powerful. even when you know what they are—believe me, there are times when I've had simple migraines when they became so overwhelming that I nearly put a bullet in my own brain to make them stop. The experience simply becomes overwhelming. It wasn't seeing the magnified floaters swarming everywhere. There was a *sound*…and a smell too. I think it's phenomenon known as kinesthesia, when the brain begins misinterpreting signals transmitted through one set of sensory channels as if they were coming from another. Everything seemed to be coming down from above, in a predatory fashion—hence Tillinghast's sensation of being hunted. It was very disturbing, as if it were triggering some deep, instinctive fear.

"I was in a highly suggestible state of mind. Panic is contagious—and the crescendo of Tillinghast's panic evidently reached such a climax that it caused blood vessels in his brain to burst. I felt…well, I suppose it was a kind of sympathetic echo of that crisis. To tell the truth, my memory of it is somewhat confused, but I really thought that I *saw* something, something alien, even though I couldn't tell what it was and have even less idea now that I have, as it were, woken up from the nightmare.

"I don't believe that I fired at any kind of monster, though. I believe that I knew that the radiation from the machine was responsible, even though the menace seemed to be suspended overhead, where I could hear that infernal weather-vane creaking away. I'm sure that I hit exactly what I was aiming at—I'm no marksman, but the range was close. I can't be sure, but I think that Tillinghast had already tried to switch off the machine…. Perhaps he couldn't find the switch, in his disturbance, or my impatience was at such a pitch that I couldn't wait for him to fumble…"

"Why do you say perhaps?" she queried, having detected some hesitation there.

I hesitated again, but she'd demanded the truth. "My impression at the time," I admitted, finally, "was that Tillinghast really had switched the machine off, but that it kept functioning regardless. It seemed still to be drawing power from the acid batteries—or at least from somewhere—but either way, whatever he did or didn't do, the machine kept running. As for the gunshot…well, that's when I blacked out. I didn't see the machine explode, so I couldn't be surprised that it had, and I don't really understand why it did. I didn't see Tillinghast collapse, either. I pulled the trigger because I just wanted it to stop, at any cost, and I think pulling the trigger was enough in itself to make me black out.

"I don't know how long I was out before I woke up, but by that time the police had arrived. God alone knows how, but someone had heard the explosion, and perhaps already telephoned to say that something unusual was happening because they'd seen the glow. Although the house is a long way from its nearest neighbor, it's on the top of a hill, and the mansard windows are visible all the way to the sea shore, and a mile inland. At any rate, the police were called, and they came out to investigate. I was still dazed when they hustled me down to their car and took me into Providence. I don't know how long I was in the holding cell either, but it was a long time—hours. The police must have sent someone to inform you in the interim, who knew that I'd been arrested but didn't know that I'd been released as soon as the facts became clear. That's it—I don't know any more."

* * * *

"I see," said Rachel, after a long pause. "Thank you, David—I know that must have been difficult, but I felt that I had to know. You're convinced, then, that the effect of the radiation was simply a matter of inducing hallucinations and delusions?"

"Yes," I said, flatly, still hoping that I really was still convinced, in spite of what I'd felt while making my tour of the house. "Given the evident kinship between the visions induced by the radiation and the sensory distortions induced by the opium in laudanum, it doesn't seem to me that there can be any rational doubt about it…but it's impossible to be rational while something like that is actually happening. Poor Tillinghast couldn't, even though he was a far more intelligent and strong-minded man than I am. Obviously, the brain can produce similar symptoms in response to electrical as well as chemical stimuli. Perhaps, as Tillinghast thought, it's an effect of the pineal body, but even if it isn't, it has to be something of that sort."

"But the effect on you was temporary?" she probed. "Those symptoms haven't lingered?"

"I've had headaches since," I confessed, uneasily. "But I had headaches before, so that's not really significant.

She must have taken note of the unease. "The reason I ask," she said, "is that I'm still puzzled by the disappearance of Gregory, Mrs. Updike and Jane. I can believe that if they suddenly began to experience hallucinations and delusions because the radiation extended much further than the attic, then they might have felt obliged to get out temporarily. But in that case, the effect should have worn off, and they would surely have come back. And if they were running around in a disorientated state, it would surely have been easy enough to pick up their trail and find out where they went…at least one of them, if not all three."

"It's a puzzle," I conceded. "But it's surely not enough to prove that they were disintegrated."

"Disintegrated?" she queried.

I remembered belatedly that I had deliberately omitted to mention what Tillinghast had said about Mrs. Updike's clothes, and was sufficiently thrown off my stride to add: "Or metamorphosed," before I could stop myself.

Fortunately, that exceeded the limits of her credulity, and she almost smiled. "Or metamorphosed," she echoed, in a tone that thought the suggestion a trifle amusing, but quite implausible. She was swift to add, though: "Is that what the members of the unholy trinity believe, do you think?"

"I doubt that they believe it," I said, "but Patterway, as a biologist, will surely be aware of the hypothesis that abnormal stimulation of the pineal gland can cause mutation and deformity. I don't know exactly what Dove's academic qualifications are, but I suspect he'll be aware of it too. If any of them has a confident theory to offer, I'm sure you'll only have to ask to get them to voice it, but believing it might be another matter. You can probably demand that they tell you everything they know, or think, simply by making it a condition of letting them see the debris of the machine. You have the relevant carrots to dangle, and you can exploit their competitiveness to your heart's content, if that's the way you want to go. Is it?"

"I don't know," she said. "I really don't know. To tell you the truth, David, I don't even know how I feel. It's been more than a week now, and the initial shock has worm off, but I really don't know how I ought to feel. Grief and sorrow, I suppose, which I do…but…it's complicated."

"You still loved him," I said, in a slightly hollow tone, knowing that she could hardly say no even if it had been true.

She did not, however, say yes. What she actually said was: "You probably think I'm a terrible person for leaving him."

"I could never think that," I assured her, with perfect honesty. "He could be difficult. I think it's much easier for a friend to ride out the kind of storms to which he was subject than for a wife, who is bound to affected more deeply and can't bounce back as easily. I can't tell you how many times he made me want to strangle him, but we both knew that it would soon blow over, and that we could give one another plenty of space until it did. Between man and wife…together round the clock…I can understand very easily why the effect and the tension built up over time, and how it might eventually have become unbearable. He could too, I think. He was deeply disappointed and hurt when you left, but I think he understood why it had happened, and even sympathized. He wasn't one for confidences of that kind, but I knew him better than anyone, and I'm certain that he didn't hold it against you. I never heard him utter a single word of criticism or malediction. If he was angry, it was with himself."

"Is that why you were angry on his behalf?" she asked, quietly.

"Me? I wasn't angry. I could never…" I stopped suddenly.

"No," she said, thoughtfully. "You couldn't, could you. So that's not why you avoided me after the separation, then? You weren't angry with me?"

I thought about denying that I'd avoided her, but decided against the lie. I contented myself with saying, "No," and hoping that she had too much tact and delicacy to ask me why, in that case, I had kept a respectful distance. Perhaps she knew, although the fact that she'd bothered to enquire as to whether I'd been angry suggested that she was at least uncertain.

She changed the subject. "What do you think I should do with the debris of the machine?" she asked. "Crisson's offered to buy it, but Patterway thinks that I owe to science and my husband's legacy to deliver it to the safe custody of Miskatonic University for what he calls scrupulous collaborative examination."

"It's hardly my place to advise you," I said.

"On the contrary," she said, "it's exactly your place. I know that I'm taking advantage of you unfairly, perhaps even cruelly, but I need guidance, and you're the one person whose guidance I can trust. If you were in my shoes, what would you do with it?"

"Chuck it in the sea," I told her, honestly. "The deeper the better… unless you need the money that Crisson's offering."

"I don't," she said. "Crawford had to help me out with my expenses while we were separated—and insisted on so doing, although I really could and perhaps should have got a job. By your standards and mine, he was almost rich, and the inheritance will allow me to live in moderate ease, either in the village or here."

"Here?"

"Why not?"

"Well…," I began, uncertain as to how I could, or should, react to that possibility.

She let me off the hook. "Do you really think that I ought to throw the remains of the machine in the sea?" she asked, and immediately went on: "Yes, of course you do, or you wouldn't have said it. But why? Do think it would be dangerous to allow Crisson or Patterway the opportunity to reconstruct it?"

"Yes, and not just to them. I've never been one of those people who think that there are things that man was not meant to know, but there really are things best avoided, and powerful hallucination machines are one of them. That one literally drove your husband mad, but he couldn't stop. He was in the grip of his passion, and…."

This time, I didn't stop because I didn't know what to say next but because Rachel interrupted me, without really meaning to, by murmuring: "His real passion."

"One of his passions," I hastened to add. "Perhaps the strongest, but not the best...obviously." I didn't spell out why it was obvious.

"So you think I ought to save Patterway and Crisson from themselves?" she said, collecting herself. "Save them from their own reckless passion, that is? But perhaps not until we've dangled the carrot, as you put it, in order to get them to tell us what they know about Crawford's work?"

I was slightly surprised to find that that was, indeed, the sum of what I'd said, without quite intending that arithmetic. I liked the way that she had said *us*, even though she probably didn't construe the meaning of the term in the same way that I did.

"Is that what you want?" I asked, warily.

"I haven't made up my mind yet," she said. "But I am curious, and if I hadn't shared Crawford's *other* passion to some extent I'd...." It was her turn to stop, although I couldn't see that there was any need to omit *I'd never have married him*...unless she was having retrospective doubts about the wisdom of that decision. But that was too optimistic, and I didn't want to draw any unjustified conclusions. There was too much at stake.

I was suddenly convinced, however, that Rachel had known perfectly well, fifteen years before, that I had been in love with her, and I strongly suspected that one of the things about which she was curious now was whether I still was, even while being uncertain of her own feelings, or how she ought to feel.

Too optimistic, I said to myself, sternly. *Don't build your hopes up too far.*

"If you don't want to throw the remains of the machine in the sea," I said, sticking to what seemed for the moment to be argumentative *terra firma*, "I don't suppose it matters much whether you give the debris to Patterway or Crisson—or Dove, come to that, if you decide that you want to spite them both. If the money really is irrelevant, you might as well toss a coin or let them draw lots for it. In all probability, nothing will come of it. A sophisticated electrical machine isn't like a mere mechanical device, easy to reassemble from its components...and from the glimpse I caught of the smithereens that police were collecting when they arrested me, the explosion did a pretty good job of rendering any reconstruction well-nigh impossible."

"But if it were you," she insisted, "you'd throw it in the sea?"

"Yes," I admitted.

"And you don't think I should move back here, to live in the house?"

I hesitated. If she moved back to the house she'd be nearer to Providence, and thus nearer to me, although we'd hardly be close neighbors. But she'd be in Tillinghast's house....

Again, I contented myself with a simple: "No."

This time, it wasn't enough.

"Why not?"

I hedged. "You have a life in New Bedford," I said. "Why abandon it?"

She knew that that was pure evasion. "Please, David," she said, in a tone that would have melted an immovable object, "I need to know. Do you think there's any danger in the house....because of the machine?"

I hesitated for a long time, but I was under compulsion to tell the truth. I couldn't refuse her that. "I don't know," I said. "Logically, there can't be, but in this instance, I'm not an objective observer. What happened that night....well, as I said, it still gives me headaches, and the jitters. It's not something I'll ever be able to forget completely, even though the memory is so vague. I'm sure it's purely subjective, and I'm sufficiently certain of that to spend tonight here...and more than one night if you still need me, but...well, I wouldn't do it for anyone but you, and the thought of your actually taking up permanent residence here...I really don't believe that you'd be in any danger, but...I'd find it disturbing. Not that that's something you need to take into account, of course."

"Of course it's something I need to take into account," she said, quietly, without specifying why or how. She paused for a few seconds before adding: "Do you feel up to going upstairs? To the attic, I mean?"

I steeled myself. "Yes," I said. I didn't add anything further, and nor did she, but I suspected that we were both echoing in our minds what I'd said about not doing it for anyone but her, and that she was weighing the implications of that remark.

"Let's go, then," she said, standing up.

She was already moving away by the time I had risen to my feet, in the direction of the first of the two staircases that would take us to Crawford Tillinghast's attic laboratory.

I took my courage in both hands, and followed her.

4

Although they had figured out soon enough that the laboratory was not, in fact, a "crime scene," the police had nevertheless made a start at gathering "evidence," and inertia had caused them to complete the task. They had sent in a municipal cleaning crew thereafter to sanitize the carpet where Tillinghast had fallen and died. The fragments of the machine had been carefully gathered into a heap and then packed into a tea-chest, presumably with the original intention of taking them away for expert examination, but once it had been decided that no crime had been committed and that the explosion had not been the result of an anarchist bomb, the chest had simply been set aside.

Rachel had picked up a lighted candle in a tray before tackling the second set of stairs, because the twilight was now fading away outside, but, somewhat to my surprise, when she flicked the switch beside the door-jamb the electric bulb in the ceiling was illuminated. I realized, on further inspection, however, that it was drawing power from the batteries and not from the generator. The light wasn't very bright and seemed a trifle unsteady, but it was adequate to permit Rachel to blow out the candle. She set the tray down on one of the work-tables, with had been tidied up, presumably by the cleaning crew, the apparatus being arranged in geometrical formations quite different from the disorder that Tillinghast had preferred.

She cast a long circular glance around the attic. I followed her example.

The cables that had connected the machine to the generator supply before Tilllinghast had decided not to employ that supply were lying loose on the floor, and the storage batteries that the scientist had employed to supply it with an alternative or additional current were still lined up in the customary stern array, the connecting cables similarly dangling. Nothing in the laboratory was glowing; there was not the slightest trace of any uncanny radiance in the room.

There were no papers in evidence; any documents contained in the laboratory had been removed, and combined with those from the study that the lawyer had forwarded to Rachel after extracting the ones he needed in order to acquit his responsibilities as the executor of the scientist's will.

Rachel continued looking around this way and that, very carefully. She inspected the wreckage of the machine with a keen gaze, although she did not remove the debris from the tea-chest, but she also examined the rest of the room scrupulously, opening the drawers in the table and examining the various items of apparatus on the shelves and tables at close range. I took a longer look into the tea-chest.

The impression I had formed while being arrested seemed to have been entirely justified. The explosion had reduced the machine to an extremely large number of fragments, only a handful of which were larger than the size of my thumb.

"Did Crawford keep a notebook in which to record his experiments?" Rachel asked me, while I was absorbed in that contemplation. "Only loose sheets were forwarded to me."

"I don't think so," I said. "I never saw him use one. I suspect that his record-keeping became rather lax in the last few months of his endeavor. Doubtless he would have written it all up, eventually, but he was too caught up in the fervor of creativity. I suspect that the vultures wouldn't find anything in the materials presently in your possession that he hadn't already communicated to his various correspondents while consulting their expertise, and probably less."

"But he talked to you about what he was doing?"

"After a fashion, but not in the last few weeks. As I told you, we'd had one of our little spats. I regret it deeply now, obviously, but you know both of us, and how we interacted…the years of your separation hadn't altered that at all. I wish I hadn't let it drag on so long, but…well, I had no idea what was going to happen, obviously, and when he sent for me, I came running. Too late, alas. Stupid. I feel guilty now."

"There's really no need," she assured me. "I do, indeed, know both of you, and I understand perfectly that removing me from the equation wouldn't have changed anything between you, except perhaps to throw you back to the behavior patterns of the period before I came into your lives. You couldn't have done anything to prevent what happened."

She was probably right. Even if I'd observed Tillinghast's obvious deterioration much earlier, what could I have done, except to urge him to stop, or at least to slow down. I had done that a hundred times before, but when had he ever taken any notice of my advice? There would just have been another spat.

"He did talk to me, before then," I agreed, getting back to the point, "but I fear that my understanding of what he tried to tell me was rather limited. Crisson would have understood what he was saying and would have known what questions to ask in order to obtain more precision, but I didn't. I fear that the private detective that Crisson appears to have hired was probably wasting his time—I doubt that there's any document here or elsewhere that would provide a vital clue to anyone seeking to replicate Crawford's work, and I'm in no position to plug that gap. He's welcome to try and bribe me if he wishes, but I really don't have anything to sell."

She didn't seem surprised my mention of the detective, and didn't query the assumption that Crisson must have been the one who had hired him. Her eyes went back to the tea-chest, but her gaze didn't seem avid with curiosity. It certainly wasn't the possible commercial value of the fragments that was on her mind.

I watched her, silently, preoccupied myself with a feeling of oddity in my head, which wasn't exactly a pain, as yet, but did not seem to bode well. I wasn't yet suffering the visual distortions that were such a frequent prelude to my migraines, but I nevertheless felt that some such disturbance commencing. I tried to reassure myself that the peril wasn't imminent, and that the symptoms might pass as soon as I was out of the attic.

"What's that noise?" Rachel asked, suddenly, with a hint of alarm in her voice. She, too, appeared to have become gradually uneasy—unsurprisingly, given the circumstances.

"It's only the weather-vane," I told her. "It's quite close at hand here, on this side of that chimney-stack. I pointed to the bare bricks of the flue that rose up in the middle of the attic floor, rudely cutting through the improvised boards, and disappeared into the slanting joists to protrude through the tiles. The place where the machine had stood during the fatal operation was almost directly underneath the place from which the sound appeared to be coming. The roof was designed in the mansard-style, with two distinct pitches, in order to offer more space within for storage or living, but Tillinghast, ever the utilitarian, had never seen fit to tack lath and plaster over the brickwork or the joists or to put wallpaper over the surface, in order to make the space look more like a conventional room, so there was nothing between us and the base of the axle of the vane, in the spaces between the roof-beams, but roofing-felt and tile.

"I thought it might be rats," she said, defensively.

"There's not so much as a mouse up here," I assured her. "No birds' nests or roosting bats." All of that was true; I did not care to think about what it might leave unmentioned, or even to wonder whether the absence might be unusual.

She had had enough procrastination. She looked me squarely in the eye and said: "*Was* there an…intruder, David?"

She meant, of course: *What was it that you were really shooting at, or thought you were shooting at?*

"I honestly don't have anything to add to what I told you downstairs," I said. "I was telling the truth, as you'd asked me to do. I was confused. I fired at the machine, because I just wanted it to stop. I won't pretend that I did it altruistically, because I could see that it was hurting Tillinghast. Yes, there were all kinds of fluid entities swarming around me, becoming more peculiar by the second, but I knew that there was no point in shooting at them."

I *was* telling the truth, so far as I knew it, But there was a nagging feeling at the back of my mind telling me, insidiously, that there was something else, something I'd deliberately forgotten, and that I might not be telling the *whole* truth.

She still seemed dissatisfied, although she didn't seem to suspect me of lying, or even of tact and delicacy.

"But Crawford saw something more than *fluid entities*," she insisted. "Something that caused his hemorrhage—something, not to put too fine a point on it, that scared him to death."

Just because it killed him, I thought but didn't say, *it doesn't mean that it was real.* Nor did I say: *And just because I don't want to believe it, it doesn't mean that it wasn't. And we really don't know, do we, exactly what effect the radiation had, let alone how, either on the ambient space or on us?*

I put the brake on that train of thought, but inertia carried it a little further forward. I had no idea, of course, what effect the radiation might have had inside Tilinghast's skull, or mine. The Medical Examiner hadn't reported any evidence of any modification to Tillinghast's brain, apart from the massive hemorrhage—but he hadn't looked for any such modification, and probably wouldn't have been able to detect anything untoward even if he had.

Rachel was still waiting for an answer, even though she hadn't actually asked a question. "I thought the machine was doing us harm," I repeated, because it seemed to be necessary, to her if not to me, for the point to be further emphasized. "Its effect was causing us to see things that weren't there. The sensation was deeply disturbing—even more so in Crawford's case, I think, than in mine, because he had exposed himself to it before. Perhaps it was foolish of me to take out the gun, but I'm sure that I hit exactly what I aimed at—although that might, in all honesty, have been an unlikelier event than my hitting the machine by accident, having fired at something else entirely."

"Do you know," she said, "it never occurred to me before how odd it is that you so rarely refer to him as Crawford, even when talking to me. I just took it for granted, as the way things had always been. Now, suddenly, it seems strange. Not that he ever called you anything but Dearden, I suppose. I was the one who always called you David."

"It's a hangover from our schooldays," I said. "There were no first names at our school. At first, after being on first-name terms as children, that seemed amusing, and we took to using our surnames invariably, with ironic emphasis at first, although it eventually became an ingrained habit. I guess we were at the impressionable age where such deep habits form. It doesn't say anything about the quality of our friendship."

"Yes it does," she said, softly. I assumed that she was reflecting on the fact that she'd always called us by our first names, just as we had always called her by hers. Was she right? I wondered. Did the fact that we'd never reverted to first-name terms say something about the quality of my friendship with Tillinghast that I'd never even suspected?

"Is that really what killed him?" she asked, getting back to the point. "Something he saw, or thought he saw?"

"How can I tell?" I countered, accurately enough. "Does it really matter what caused the intensity of his reaction?"

Of course it mattered, if there was the slightest possibility that what he saw had been real, material and menacing—but she let the rhetorical question stand without protest. She was looking into my eyes, as if trying to read my mind. What she saw, I couldn't tell, beyond the obvious—but I felt, as I looked into her eyes, that I could see grief therein, and an irreducible residue of love and regret. It *did* matter to her how and why Tillinghast had died. She wanted to know, because she wanted to know how to feel about it, and she thought—perhaps mistakenly, but who can tell?—that not knowing exactly what had killed him was somehow preventing her from knowing exactly how she felt about it.

It occurred to me, suddenly, that she blamed herself. She was thinking that if she had not left her husband—that if she had stuck to her marriage vows and stayed with him no matter what—perhaps he would never even have built the accursed machine…or even if he had, if she had still been living with him, that she would have been able to save him, somehow, from its dire effects.

Perhaps, I thought, she was right.

"It was my fault," I told her, feeling that I ought at least to share her burden. "I should have been there to see what was happening to him in the weeks before he gave me that final demonstration. I should have known, even before we had the spat, that it was leading to disaster. I should have stopped him. I had every opportunity. You didn't."

"But you didn't have the means," she said, her voice hardly more than a whisper. "No, David, it wasn't your fault, or mine. He was a grown man—in his forties, for God's sake—fully responsible for himself."

But it was painfully obvious that she thought that she had had a share of that responsibility: a share that she had voluntarily abandoned by leaving him. There didn't seem to be any point in arguing against that, so I changed the subject, once again reverting to seemingly firmer ground.

"The *machine* was responsible for his death," I told her, insistently. "Maybe I can't be sure exactly how, but there's no doubt about it. That's not going to stop Crisson wanting to buy the pieces, though, or Patterway wanting to get them into the laboratories at Miskatonic for painstaking investigation, or Dove wanting to charm himself into some kind of collaboration with either or both of them. Nor will it stop them if the pieces prove unhelpful and there are no specific plans, in all probability—they'll just take the view that it will take them a little longer to duplicate the work, starting from an earlier stage."

"They're grown men too," she said. "Patterway's older than Crawford, Dove must be almost the same age, and Crisson only four or five years younger. They're entitled to be the architects of their own fate—and they've already had a demonstrative warning, even if they didn't have the front row seat that you did."

She was right. I went with the flow. "Perhaps you should hand everything over to one or all of them and wish them luck, if you don't want to chuck the scrap metal in the sea," I said, judging that to be what she wanted probably me to say, by way of endorsement. "But the one thing you shouldn't do is involve yourself in any investigation any of them carries out. I understand that you want to know, and I think I understand why, but it really would be wiser to wash your hands of the whole business, one way or another." *If you can*, I added, silently

She nodded slowly—but only to indicate that she understood, not that she had come to a decision. She relaxed her stare, though, and she too made a bid for safer ground.

"Thank you for being here, David," she said. "Alone, I'm not sure that I'd have had the strength…."

She looked around again, searching the lighted space for evidence of ominous presence. The electric bulb was far brighter and steadier than the candle she had blown out, but the mansard was large, and still had shadowed corners, and the bulb itself was not as constant in its output of light as I could have wished. It seemed to be making a tiny sound, somewhere between a sizzle and hum, which wasn't quite drowned out by the insistent creaking of the weather-vane. The latter seemed unable to make up its mind exactly which way the wind was blowing.

On the whole, though, I felt proud of myself. Rachel was glad I was here, and that was enough for me to be glad that I was here. She wouldn't have wanted to be alone here, and that was more than enough for me to want, not merely that she shouldn't be, but that I should be the one standing between her and isolation. Even if my head had started pounding full tilt, and even if ominous shapes had actually begun to stir restlessly in the shadows, I would still have been glad, because I was her knight in not-so-shining armor, and I would have been glad to face any kind of monsters on her behalf.

That told me, I suppose, that I could be utterly confident of my own feelings in her regard, which had obviously emerged from their long eclipse as powerfully radiant as ever. But what about hers? How much could I and ought I to read into the fact that she didn't want to be alone here, and that she was so relentlessly intent on interrogating me repeatedly as to the exact circumstances of her husband's death.

For the moment, she said, she didn't know how she felt. That was fair enough. It only meant that she needed time, and perhaps a little guidance. I was prepared to give her all the time she needed, and all the guidance I could, no matter what the risk. That was what my situation demanded. That was what sanity demanded. And if hallucinations, or even monsters, came to threaten that demand, I simply had to be strong. For once in my life, I had to be better than a coward.

But deep down, I was shivering. I didn't know why, but I was. One way or another, the accursed machine had left lingering effects in me, or in the house, or in both of us. Like the coward I was, I was scared without knowing why.

Perhaps, I thought, Patterway, Crisson, or even Dove, could explain it. Would that help, I wondered, or would it have the opposite effect? Time would tell, presumably, and fairly soon, now.

Rachel was thinking about the time too.

"Let's go back down," she said. "I'm hungry, aren't you? Stephen should have been back with the supplies long ago, and Emily's a tolerable cook...tolerable in every capacity, in fact." She didn't have to explain why the servants' presence didn't count, in terms of her being—or feeling—alone.

"Yes," I said, "best get something to eat, ready for the vultures' landing."

"Are they really vultures?" she queried. She meant rather than passionate scholars, all too human.

"Jackals?" I suggested, as a potential alternative.

"Let's hope so," she said. "I wouldn't want them turning into Hydes."

I laughed, although, as macabre wordplay went, it really didn't seem to be very funny.

"Shall I bring the tea-chest down?" I asked.

She seemed to weigh up the pros and cons. "No," she said, finally. "Let's leave it where it is. There'll be time to fetch it, if it needs to be fetched. First, I want to make the vultures sing—or the jackals howl—before I make a decision as to whether or not I ought to turn over the fragments. Whatever I decide, I won't have any conscience about it. They're the ones who wanted to come. I'd have been quite content to let things lie."

I wasn't entirely convinced by that, but I decided to believe it. Chivalry demanded it.

* * * *

Having survived the attic laboratory unscathed, I felt that I was holding up well, fully capable of playing the knight all night, if necessary—but I was overconfident. Absurd as it may seem, it was the dinner that seemed to do the damage.

Not that there was anything wrong with the preparation of the food, which was pedestrian but competent, or even the choice of menu, which was predictable enough and quite familiar…but there was *something* about it that had a triggering effect.

Stephen had done what everyone in the state tends to do when shopping for a meal to be eaten the same day, and had bought fresh seafood—not cod, which was still considered commonplace even though the fish themselves no longer arrived at the Grand Banks every year in vast profusion, nor lobster, which was also considered a trifle vulgar, but herring and octopus. I had eaten both of them hundreds of times before, sometimes even in the same meal, and had never feared either, although I had the normal anxieties regarding mussels and oysters—but not all octopodes are alike, it seems. Indeed, if I judged correctly, in spite of its careful slicing, the one of which I ate the greater share must have had more than eight limbs; I almost commented on it, wondering aloud whether a ten-tentacled octopus might have the same status as a good luck charm as a four-leafed shamrock, but refrained. Perhaps I had a premonition that the effect might be opposite…if the octopus really was the guilty party.

At any rate, I had hardly finished drinking my coffee when I began to feel ill—not merely odd, but genuinely ill. I began to see the floaters too.

I had consulted my doctor about the migraines and their hallucinatory spinoff, of course, and he had eventually referred me to a specialist ophthalmologist, who had taken the usual hobby-horse rider's delights in explaining to me a great length what was going on. He had assured me that visual phenomena often preceded migraines, and that recent study had begun produced an elaborate classification of them. He waxed lyrical about floaters—that was the term he used, and seemed delighted that I had come up with it independently—and gave me an uncannily accurate description of their appearance and behavior without my giving him any substantial hints in advance. He had been duly proud of the acumen of his science when I had confirmed his observations.

"Is it really normal for them to appear to pass through walls and other solid objects?" I had asked him.

"But of course," he had replied. "They're an illusion conjured up by your brain; they have no need to obey the laws of solid-state physics, or those of optics. They're phantoms. I have patients who suffer much worse, believe me. When people begin to lose their sight, because of the deterioration of the retina or the clouding of the cornea, the brain often substitutes for the lack of information received by producing hallucinations far more complex than yours—sinister enough, merely by virtue of their unreality, even when the imaginary objects are perfectly ordinary, but they often seem menacing, even monstrous."

"Monstrous?" I repeated, perhaps overlooking the more genuinely ominous suggestion that I might have begun to lose my eyesight. "How monstrous?"

"I suspect that depends on the personality of the individual. None of us has an entirely clear conscience, alas, and our poor brains are sometimes at the mercy of our fears—sometimes fears that go back to childhood, and have simply been lying dormant for decades. You have no need to worry unduly yet, though. Having just passed forty, you're beginning to suffer from the presbyopic effects of a hardened lens and the fact that the muscles controlling it are getting weaker—that's why you're more prone to suffer disturbing effects late in the day, when the eye-muscles get tired—and the fact that you've always been congenitally short-sighted means that the developing long-sightedness is causing you particular confusions as your natural field of focus narrows drastically. I can't see any other signs of physical deterioration, though:

no glaucoma, no cataracts, no retinal detachment. There's just the migraines, so far. When they begin to come on, you need to lie down in a dark room and keep still. I'll give you a new prescription that will help numb the effects."

By a "new prescription," of course, he meant something other than the laudanum that my own physician has prescribed, but he was short of options, except for suggesting different sedatives. He began with chloral hydrate and then moved on to tincture of cannabis—but having tried them both, neither seemed as effective as laudanum, so I had eventually reverted to using that as my main line of defense. The ophthalmologist had urged me to keep two treatments close at hand, and give the milder one a chance before moving on to the stronger one. He also told me to beware of the fact that the cannabis, like the laudanum, might encourage more vivid hallucinations on occasion, even while numbing the pain. I had followed his instructions in a desultory fashion—on coming out to Tillinghast's house I had packed the chloral as well as laudanum in my valise, not wanting to be caught away from home by embarrassing symptoms without the option of employing *force majeure* against them, but I had no real intention of using the chloral if things got bad, no matter what risk there was in encouraging more vivid hallucinations.

"I'm truly sorry," I said to Rachel, when the floaters began to swarm more aggressively. "I know that there's not much time before the vultures gather, but I really need to lie down for a few minutes, in order to dispel the preliminary symptoms of a headache. I promise that I'll be ready and able to lend you any support you might need by the stroke of eight, when the vultures descend, but in order to be able to do that, I need to get my body and brain under control, and the only way to do that is by means of careful self-discipline."

"Of course," she said. "Poor David—have *you* been working too hard?"

In fact, I had hardly been working at all for more than a fortnight. Although we schoolteachers always claim that the notion that the long summer break is pure holiday is a myth, we are mostly trying to conceal our indolence. I had not opened a book or picked up a pen since the end of July. Fortunately, Rachel took my denial as a further sign of heroic modesty.

* * * *

I retired to the bedroom to which Rachel had referred, probably with less significance that I wanted to attach to the phrase, as my "old room." It was directly above Tillinghast's study, and when I lay down with a blindfold over my eyes, attempting perfect stillness, I could hear her rummaging through the drawers of the desk and the filing-cabinet, each of which made an individually-distinguishable creak as it opened and closed. I could tell that she was being thorough, but she was merely being methodical, not feverish. She wasn't searching with the avid determination that the jackals would have brought to the task, eager to fall upon some scrap of paper containing a hopefully-crucial wiring-diagram or list of instrument-settings. She had always been a neat and orderly housekeeper while she was living in the house—habits carried over, I assumed, from her earlier career as a laboratory technician.

As the migraine developed, however, I soon lost interest in creaks from the study, and Rachel's subsequent movements as she continued to take inventory of her shabby inheritance. No matter how hard I tried to instruct my brain to see only what my eyes registered as really present, the floaters persisted to swim around the inner space of my mind.

Had I not been wearing the blindfold, I knew, I would have seen them moving back and forth through the walls and ceiling of my room—and also moving through the bed, my own body, and one another. When they seemed to be paradoxically present in the three-dimensional world revealed to sight, they often gave the impression of being living things, akin to sea-creatures—more often jellyfish and sea-cucumbers than cephalopods or fish, but not obedient to any very rigid system of classification. Exiled to the dark behind my eyes, however, they seemed more alien than that, as if they were no longer completely defined by their shapes, or any resemblance to earthly species.

Perhaps it is absurd to say so—the most bizarre of all my hallucinations—but I was beginning to conceive of the inner spaces of my mind not as a three-dimensional space analogous to the framework implied and constructed by the sense sight, but as something more complex and convoluted. I deemed that absurd because, after all, we have no other way of imagining any space other than by analogy with the model created by sight but it was nevertheless the way I felt. I say "created by sight" rather than "perceived by sight" because one has to maintain a certain intellectual awareness of the difference between the phenomenal and noumenal worlds, even if perception will not allow us to be aware of any. Intellectual respectability demands Kantian doubt, lest we surrender to the mere brutality of sensory tyranny; we are human, after all.

Even so, the mere awareness of the theoretical possibility of other modes of sensory perception should not be enough to allow us to imagine them. Conceiving of the *idea* of a fourth dimension, or any kind of multidimensional plenum of parallel worlds, cannot be enough to allow us to imagine such a fourth dimension or some such plenum inside our heads, whether we are dreaming or focusing our attention as intently as possible, because the analogical apparatus simply is not there…or should not be there.

And yet…when my eyes were firmly closed, and the illusory floaters produced by my malfunctioning brain were exiled to a purely theoretical space, where they could no longer mimic creatures of the sea, I began to imagine that I could see *beyond* their shape, into the dimensions of which those apparent shapes were mere cross-sections, and that in seeing them in that augmented fashion, I could see the imaginary space in which they seemed to be framed as something more, something more far-reaching, something far more complex.

The idea that worlds parallel to our own exist had been a source of fascination for Tillinghast long before he had conceived the project of designing and building his accursed machine, so I had often heard him talk about it. Indeed, he had made several concerted efforts over the years to explain it and justify it to me, even though he considered me, as a non-scientist, incapable of appreciating the logic and the beauty of the notion.

Initially, as even I could see was only logical, he had waxed lyrical about the imitation of the five senses—or "the one sense," as he was sometimes fond of saying, on the grounds that sight, hearing, smell and taste were all, essentially, varieties of touch. He seemed to find it easy enough to imagine that there might be other potential senses, which were not varieties of touch, allowing intuition without any kind of crude physical contact, by substances, waves or chemicals, and which might give us psychological access to other categories of entities living in parallel with us.

"Such entities," he had once said, "would not be able to interact with us physically, in the ordinary way, but if we could perceive them, they would be able to act upon us psychologically, and hence psychosomatically. They might be able to produce within us the total illusion of materiality"

"That sounds very uncomfortable," I had observed, if my memory serves me right.

"Perhaps it would be," he said, "but perhaps it might be rewarding too. It's not impossible that we have such latent senses, and that they once played a more considerable role in the mental lives of our remote ancestors, but atrophied somewhat as our ancestral species came to rely more and more on the varieties of the touch sense, which must have been more pragmatic and utilitarian then, in a perennially hostile environment. Now that we have acquired more authority over that environment, however, and our survival is more easily guaranteed, perhaps the existential scope has opened up again for the redevelopment of the other senses. Perhaps they do become operative sometimes, in some individuals."

"Thus accounting for sightings of ghosts?" I suggested. "Not to mention incubi and succubi, sirens and demons."

"And angels," he added. "Let's not forget the more benign possibilities."

He never had, it seems. I recalled his insistence that his "pets" were harmless even while they were in the process of scaring him to death, and delivering his servants either to panic flight, disintegration, or….who knows what?

Obviously—or, at least, it seemed obvious to me—that was why he had made contact with Lyman Dove, the supposed expert on apparitions and supersensory abilities, as well as with Crisson, the expert on exotic electrical machinery, the disciple of Nikola Tesla, Tesla himself being presumably out of reach. But Patterway? A biologist? That implied something more substantial. Or did it? Was it still merely a matter of psychological and psychosomatic effects, or also an interest in the physiology of the psychosomatic effects concerned….the effects that might, in extreme case, tend to metamorphoses?

Given the region in which we lived, of course we had all heard tales of strange metamorphoses, especially in connection with such ill-reputed locations as Dunwich and Innsmouth. Presumably, I would find out, if Rachel was going to demand that her three guests told their stories before she would even consider allowing one or more of them access to the fragments of the machine…provided that I could get rid of the damned floaters before they developed into a full-blown migraine and reduced me to complete helplessness.

That could not happen. Rachel needed me.

My thoughts, inevitably, went to the chloral and the laudanum in my valise. Perhaps, if I were to take the milder drug, it might prevent the further development of the migraine. On the other hand, even chloral might intensify the tendency to hallucination. Given that simply being in the house already seemed to be having an influence on that tendency, it might to be wise to encourage it further. Darkness had fallen outside now, and there was no electric light, except in the attic laboratory, where the bulb was connected to the acid batteries. Candlelight, by its very nature, and even the light of oil lamps, was likely to be far more conducive to unease, and hence to conceptual errors, than the broad daylight of late summer.

Nor was it merely the floaters, for optical fictions were no longer the only premonitory symptoms of my headaches. The auditory phenomena had initially manifested themselves as a commonplace "ringing in the ears" of the kind that many people experience from time to time, but my particular "ring" was more akin to a hiss, and its sibilance was easy aided by an excited imagination to take on the semblance of a whisperer, muttering unintelligible words that had something of the implication of magical invocations.

I knew full well that the whisper I could hear at the moment was merely the effect of being in a relatively unfamiliar bedroom in a relative unfamiliar location, whose dominant sound was not the traffic noises that formed the sonic background of my town house but the relentless creaking of the weather-vane above the house, which seemed quite incapable of resting in a single direction.

The house, although some distance from the sea, was inevitably subject to breezes in the morning and evening, as the relative temperate of the sea and the land changed with the initial exposure to the sun and the fall of darkness, and I knew that such breezes were notoriously unsteady, but even so, the creaking of the weather-vane seemed excessive to me. Perhaps a dab of grease or a drop of oil would diminish the intensity of the shrill sound considerably, but if it had been up to me, I would simply have the damn thing taken down, all the more so as it probably increased the likelihood that the house might be struck by lightning during one of the sudden storms that often blew up at this time of year, and I had no faith in its ability to double effectively as a lightning-conductor.

For some reason, the attic above my head did not diminish the filtered sound of the weather-vane at all, but actually seemed to amplify it, like the echo-chamber of a stringed instrument, and although the attic was carpeted, that did not seem to have a muffling effect either.

It would have been kinder, in a way, if I had been able to make out what the insidious whisper was actually trying to say—because it really did seem, in my imagination, to be making an effort toward meaning and clarity, however ineffectual. It remained stubbornly incomprehensible, however, as if it were coming from another world, or as if, instead of being produced by the vocal cords, tongue and lips of a human being, the sounds were being produced by some metamorphosite that was attempting to speak English without the necessary apparatus to produce the appropriate phonemes.

Perhaps, I thought, it was Gregory or Mrs. Updike, attempting to issue a dire warning to me from wherever they had been taken by

Crawford Tillighast's "pets"—but immediately thereafter, I thought that that was exactly the sort of thing I ought not to be thinking, lest it add psychological fuel to the hallucinatory effects that I was already experiencing.

It is, however, notoriously difficult to avoid thinking about topics once one has formed the resolution of avoid them, because the thought of their avoidance is self-defeating. I did not take the blindfold off to look at my watch, but I was certain, or at least almost certain, that the clock downstairs must be about to strike eight: the hour for which the three jackals had been invited, in order to pay the price of their temptation by telling Rachel what she wanted to know about her husband's ideas and research, so that she might at least comprehend the death about which she did not yet know exactly how she felt.

Floaters or no floaters, I thought, I was going to have to go downstairs when the bell outside the front door rang, or the chock chimed eight, which ever happened first. Even if taking off the blindfold and moving around the house made it more likely that the migraine would develop more fully, I would have to fight it, to tolerate the torture without breaking, because Rachel needed my moral support and I dare not let her down, because it was not inconceivable that my own future—perhaps it would not be to much of an exaggeration to say my life—might depend on my ability to provide that moral support and serve as her protector against the predatory scholars. Even if the whispers were slyly trying to taunt me with the threat of failure in that endeavor, I had to try. I had to be brave. I had to pull myself together.

But the distant clock did not chime and the distant doorbell did not ring, while the seconds went by. The cliché holds that seconds of that nature seem like centuries, but they did not; they only seemed to be seconds, filling no more time than usual, but still I was having difficult progressing from ne to the next, as if I were weary of time itself, no longer able to cope with it's natural rhythm…and there were so many of them.

But then the doorbell *did* ring, and immediately afterwards, the chock chimed. And I had to get up, like an automaton, even though the floaters were still there, no longer haunting the artificial void behind the blindfold but moving through the candle-lit air of the room, and passing through the walls.

I tried to keep my gait steady as I went downstairs, but it wasn't easy, and I longed to be able to sit down in the drawing room, perhaps on the sofa with Rachel, so that we could confront the enemy together, shoulder to shoulder.

5

As I had imagined, and hoped, Rachel had arranged the furniture in the drawing room so that the three visitors were seated on dining chairs in a row facing the sofa, where Rachel and I were ensconced. She wanted to address them with a preliminary speech laying down what she considered to be the rules of the meeting, but she was, perhaps not surprisingly, interrupted before she had even started, by Robert Crisson, who, instead of taking the seat indicated to him, whipped a sheaf of papers out of the brown leather briefcase he was carrying and brandished them like a weapon or a regimental standard.

"It might save us all a great deal of time," he said, "If you will listen to my proposition. I have a contract here, drawn up in full detail, by which, if Mrs. Tillinghast cares to sign it, she will sell me this house, all of its movable contents, all of its dependencies and the adjacent land, for a price twenty-five per cent above its expertly-appraised value."

The announcement was obviously news to Patterway and Dove as well as to Rachel and me, and something of a bombshell. Patterway, who had already sat down, jumped to his feet again, and uttered a strangled protest. Crisson, who considered that he had the floor, gestured to him to wait. Patterway was a short, plump, balding man, whereas Crisson was tall, still in the prime of life, with the bearing of a man used to giving orders and having them obeyed. Patterway had no chance of asserting himself.

"One moment," Crisson said, loftily. "I haven't finished. Obviously, the sale cannot go through immediately, because the house, although it is undoubtedly Mrs. Tillinghast's property, will remain in a legal limbo of sorts until the will has gone through the probate progress and has been fully and officially executed. It will therefore be impossible for me to take possession of the house and its contents for several more days—perhaps weeks, given the glacial pace of legal bureaucracy in this particular backwater of the United Sates. Nevertheless, if Mrs. Tillinghast cares to sign the document now—I believe we have sufficient witnesses present for me not to have to summon my chauffeur from the Cadillac—it will include an undertaking not to dispose of any of the assets in that inconvenient interim, but to reserve them for my exclusive use as and when full legal possession becomes feasible.

"That will not, of course, prevent Mrs. Tillinghast and Mr. Dearden from giving any verbal information that they are ready and willing to impart this evening to whomsoever they wish, but all artifacts and documents previously belonging to Crawford Tillinghast must be held at my discretion, and not displaced without my permission. I believe, Mrs. Tillinghast, that you will find the financial terms of the offer very acceptable, not to say generous."

With a veritable flourish, he handed the documents he was waving to Tillinghast's widow, who accepted them, but made no attempt to read them. She deposited them on a side-table and replied, with the utmost calm:

"I shall consider your kind offer in due course, Mr. Crisson, but I fear that you might have mistaken the significance of the invitation I made to you all. I did not ask you here in order to give you, or even to sell you, information regarding my late husband's work, but merely to ask you for it."

It was Crisson's turn to look thunderstruck. Patterway, by contrast, smiled, and Lyman Dove did not seem at all displeased to see Crisson thwarted so coolly. Patterway took his seat again of his own accord—Dove had never left his—but Crisson had to be ordered to sit down by an imperious gesture on Rachel's part. He did; she had seized control of the situation.

"I don't understand," Crisson said. "I thought...."

"That you were here for some kind of auction?" Rachel said. "Not at all. The letters commiserating me on my loss that you all wrote me so kindly, and so promptly, gave me to understand that you had been in correspondence with my late husband, and must therefore have had some familiarity with his ideas, or some aspect thereof. As you doubtless know, my husband and I had been living apart for some time, and I had fallen somewhat out of touch with his work. I thought that the pooling of the knowledge that the three of you possess might enable me to acquire—belatedly, I admit—some insight into my husband's recent work, and the circumstances that led to his death. I thought that you might benefit yourselves from such a pooling of information, all the more so if my good friend Mr. Dearden, who was with Crawford when he died, added the scant information in his possession to the pool. Once we are all more fully informed, it might be possible for me to consider in a reasonable and responsible fashion, what ought to be done with the...legacy...of my husband's endeavors."

Having heard that explanation, Crisson seemed more defiant than dismayed; he was doubtless annoyed by what he considered to be procrastination, but he had not lost confidence in the power of his money—a confidence that Patterway, at least clearly did not share, having made his own measure of Rachel's tone and manner, and having maintained his own optimism with regard to the possibility of adding Tillinghast's scientific legacy to Miskatonic's exotic treasure-trove.

Dove simply seemed amused, and he was the one to break the silence. "What an excellent idea," he said. "I congratulate you, Mr. Tillinghast, on your good sense and good manners. I find your plan delightful, as I'm sure that my…competitors do. The prize that we are after is, of course, enlightenment, and you seem to have mapped out the ideal road for us to follow."

The speech was clearly intended to be elegant and eloquent, but for myself, I thought it lacked the charm of which he had earlier boasted. On the other hand, I was attempting with all my might to sit perfectly still and to ignore the troublesome floaters, in the hope that they might go away, so I was not in any condition to weigh such intangibles as charm accurately.

"Indeed," said Patterway, swiftly, in order to demonstrate to Crisson that he was in a minority of one. "Most acceptable."

Crisson shrugged. "I have no objection to the procedure," he conceded, ungraciously.

"Excellent," said Rachel. "Would you care to start, Professor Patterway?" She shot a sideways glance of self-satisfaction at me. I tried to muster an appropriately encouraging smile.

"If you wish," said the man from Miskatonic, shifting in his chair in order to assume the most comfortable stance for narration. "As you know from my letter, Mrs. Tillinghast, I was not in correspondence with your husband for very long, but I hope that our rapid exchange of ideas was useful to him, and it has been for me. I shall not go to into an elaborate account of the Miskatonic expeditions that brought back certain previously-unseen artifacts and documents from Asia, South America and Antarctica, or the unexpected connections that we have been able to draw between those artifacts, as they have been reported, albeit superficially, in the press. They have even begun to inspire works of fiction—of which many of my colleagues disapprove, but which I find rather fascinating.

"Suffice it to say that some of the documents in question, in combination with stone artifacts and folklore collected from various populations, not all primitive, suggest that the Earth was visited, or perhaps invaded, in the remote past by a number of extraterrestrial entities that involved themselves temporarily in the direction of Earthly evolution, including human evolution, but then became inactive, as a result of internecine conflicts.

"Some of those entities, it seems, were subsequently worshiped by various human tribes as gods, and became the object of various rites of religious and magical invocation—rites that are thought by some commentators not to be entirely without effect, because some of these entities, although dormant in remote locations on earth, or removed to spaces displaced in other dimensions, are still able to bring about effects therefrom in the right circumstances. Most of those effects seem to be mental, including dreams and hallucinations of a horrible and terrifying nature, but there are reports, which might conceivably be more than merely anecdotal, of complex and rather loathsome physical metamorphoses.

"Having read accounts of our findings in the newspapers—hostile and mocking accounts, as is unfortunately usual in such reportage, and not merely in the relentlessly anti-intellectual yellow press—Dr. Tillinghast was able to read between the lines and discern that there might be some truth in the summary that I have just given you. That is something, I fear, that exceeds the imagination of many of my colleagues, who regard the materials simply as a collection of myths, perhaps complimentary to the vivid and phantasmagorical imagination of certain prehistoric peoples, but of no value as evidence.

"Having taken note of the use in the reportage of the word 'extraterrestrial,' which the reporter in question took to mean that it implied an origin on some other planet in the solar system, or a world orbiting a distant star, Dr. Tillinghast wrote to ask for my opinion of the hypothesis that the source of the entities in question might be some kind of parallel dimension akin to the one to which at least one such entity is said to have been banished, and perhaps even imprisoned.

"Dr. Tillinghast explained to me that he had begun experiments involving the stimulation of the pineal body in the brain by means of penetrating radiation, with the aim of enhancing dormant senses that would allow us to perceive entities in our surroundings us that are normally invisible and intangible. He reported that he had contrived by that means to perceive numinous entities of an essentially inoffensive nature so far as material beings are concerned, although predatory with regard to one another. He was hoping, over time, to build up an elaborate account of their pseudo-biology and ecology.

"In the process of that observational program, however, Dr. Tillinghast told me that he began to see *further*, as it were, than the perceptible spaces that surround us, into regions displaced from our everyday space in other dimensions than the three familiar to our sight: spaces *beyond* our space, seemingly inhabited by much more complex and much more peculiar entities. Like the numinous beings that surround us—if Dr. Tillinghast's observations are to be trusted—the inhabitants of those exotic dimensions cannot normally perceive or interact with the inhabitants of our space, but he believed that, just as the radiations he had discovered had permitted him, at length, to glimpse them and their universe, it had also permitted them to perceive him and ours.

"Dr. Tillinghast did not think, at least initially, according to the communications he made to me, that the entities he glimpsed in that further beyond are hostile. He did suggest to me, however, that they certainly seemed curious, and speculated that their curiosity might be a greater danger than active malevolence, as our scientific curiosity often is to tiny creatures that we undertake to study. As he said in one of his letters, there can be no direr fate for an ant than to fall into the hands of an inquisitive and experimentally-inclined entomologist.

"That was the situation when our correspondence was interrupted. I am very curious to know whether the entities he glimpsed, if they were in fact real, had anything to do with his death, or with the disappearance of his servants, as reported in the press. I would also be very curious to see any research notes Dr. Tillinghast might have made regarding the nature and behavior of these entities, and, obviously, any information he recorded regarding his means of generating and deploying his newly-discovered radiation. Clearly, that generation and deployment, if his experiments are to be repeated and continued, need to be handled with the utmost care, by intelligent and responsible individuals who will not make reckless use of the…"

"Ha!" Crisson put in, rudely. "You have the nerve to call those dullards and crackpots at Miskatonic intelligent and responsible? You have very low standards, my friend."

"Such terms are inherently relative, sir," Patterway retorted, more than a trifle waspishly, "but if we are to make comparisons, I would far rather trust the intelligence and responsibility of my colleagues at the university than a wealthy dabbler in science who takes such a pride in his supposed intellectual independence that he would far rather be wrong than orthodox."

Dove laughed. Rachel made placatory gestures. She was quick to say: "Have you anything further to add, Professor?"

"No," said Patterway, "that's the gist of it. I am, of course willing to make the full content of Dr. Tillinghast's letters available to you, Mrs. Tillinghast, as I consider that you have a natural moral right to see them...but I think that it will be otherwise appropriate to respect their confidentiality. Your turn, *Mr.* Crisson."

"I do, in fact, have a doctorate," Crisson said, loftily, "from a far better university than Miskatonic, but I don't make a fetish out of using the title. I fear that the bulk of my own correspondence with Dr. Tillinghast would be incomprehensible to the layman, being concerned with the theory and mathematics of various kinds of radiation and exotic electrical phenomena, but I am perfectly willing to show it to you, Mrs. Tillinhghast, if it would be of any assistance to you in the advancement of your learning. Naturally, I have the same concerns regarding appropriate confidentiality as the worthy professor, so I would be reluctant to expose the content more generally.

"Unfortunately, our correspondence was relatively brief, and mostly concerned with theoretical matters. I am, however, convinced that, had he not been overtaken by unfortunate circumstances, Dr. Tillinghast would have given me the full specifications of his machine, and would very probably have entered into collaboration with me in order to design better ones, to the construction of which I could have lent my abundant technical expertise—expertise, I ought to stress, that no one at Miskatonic possesses.

"Dr. Tillinghast and I did, however, exchange some ideas regarding the hallucinations from which he was beginning to suffer, and which he was inclined to attribute to some kind of 'impurities' in the radiation that he was generating. He wanted my advice on cleaning up, as it were, his generating process, in order to produce a clearer and more focused sight of our space and others, devoid of unhelpful emotional intrusions that detracted from the scientific objectivity of the observation. Had we been able to do that, he might well have avoided the unfortunate accident that resulted in his unfortunate death and the tragic destruction of the machine."

Rachel glanced at me, having taken due note of the fact that, so far as Crisson was concerned, her husband's death was merely "unfortunate," while the destruction of his machine was "tragic." I felt incapable of speech, but I hope that my expression was suitably sympathetic.

"What did my husband mean by 'impurities' in his radiation?" she asked.

"That is an interesting question," Crisson said, "and one that I had looked forward to discussing with him. You're obviously aware that sunlight is a complex combination of electromagnetic radiations of different wavelengths, not only amenable to being divided by the prism into different colors but also containing invisible wavelengths beyond both the red end of the visual spectrum and the violet. The radiation that Tillinghast was endeavoring to produce belonged to a different genre than the electromagnetic, and should, in theory, have been invisible, but it was not. It produced a kind of violet glow, but which, on analysis, did not have the usually wavelength of violet light. Tillinghast hypothesized that it was, in fact, ultraviolet radiation that had somehow been transformed, or metamorphosed by its association with what might well be called Tillinghast radiation in future.

"He suggested that it might well be the consequence of some such combination of his own radiation with electromagnetic 'impurities' that permitted the entities he called semi-fluid to become visible. He was interested in the possibility of 'purifying' his radiation, so as to dispose of the inconvenient sight of the semi-fluid entities belonging to our own universe, but in order to do that, he needed a better theoretical understanding of the nature of both genres of radiation, and the whole range of possibilities associated with their combination. It was a fascinating field of research, and the prospect of taking part it in made me extremely eager to see the machine and to built others of a similar type. That's why I consider its accidental destruction to be a uniquely terrible tragedy."

"Was it really an accident?" Dove asked, glancing in my direction. "I'd like to clarify that with Mr. Dearden, if possible. I'd like to be certain as to whether he actually meant to hit the machine, or whether he was firing at something else and either missed or sent his bullet clean through his target. That datum would have a considerable effect on our interpretation of the event and its backcloth, would it not?" Diplomatically, he did not mention having already asked me the question once before.

"Mr. Dearden will take his turn at explanation," Rachel cut in. "Perhaps, Mr. Dove, you'd care to lay your own cards on the table first, so to speak, and inform us as to the nature of your correspondence with my late husband."

Dove shrugged. "If you wish," he said. "He wrote to me asking whether I had any information regarding a particular class of apparition, including floating globular and numinous objects capable of passing through solid walls, and horrible chimeras combining aspects of the cephalopodan, the coelenterate and the insectile. I was able to provide him with a small number of exoteric references, and some esoteric ones based on my personal research in the archives of the Societé Harmonique de Paris, which have not yet been made public. There is some material therein that might be a useful supplement to the Miskatonic database on which Professor Patterway and his colleagues have been laboring so determinedly for some years, also without any sign yet of detailed scientific publication, although rumor inevitably abounds.

"I was struck not only by Dr. Tillinghast's initial determination to believe that the entities he had glimpsed, or believed that he had glimpsed, were not hostile to humankind—an assertion that has been echoed by my two estimable colleagues—and seems to me to be a strange species of defiant optimism. In my replies, I informed him that the data I have collected strongly implies that such apparitions are indeed inimical, and that the experience of centuries seems to indicate that any glimpses that are caught of such entities, and any attempts to invoke them, very often end disastrously, with either insanity or death.

"In fairness, I ought to say that my research also suggests that Professor Patterway is correct, and his colleagues wrong, about the real, if somewhat elusive, existence of the entities to which the Miskatonic documents are alleged to refer. They are not mere figments of the pre-literate imagination. For that reason, I am afraid, if not absolutely convinced, that the things that Tilinghast perceived were not mere hallucinations, but real entities, and that they were indeed dangerous. I tried to warn Dr. Tillinghast that if he continued to make observations by means of the radiation generated by his machine, he would by courting disaster. I was unimpressed by his apparent fascination with the notion of 'impurities' in the radiation, which seemed to me to be irrelevant to the real issue.

"I tried to persuade your husband, Mrs. Tillinghast, that if he continued to expose himself and his apparatus to the inquisitive attention of hyperdimensional beings, his doom was almost certain, but he did not want to believe me. I take no pleasure in being proved right in such a horrid fashion, and I feel strongly that there is a real danger in surrendering the remnants of his machine to men of science determined to duplicate it and to supplement his observations. If I were you, Mrs. Tillinghast, I would complete their destruction, and if my correspondence with your husband might contribute to proving that necessity to you, I will be glad to give you access to it, on the same terms of restricted confidentiality that my colleagues have offered. To sell the debris for money, as you have been crudely tempted to do, would, in my opinion, be a gross failure of moral responsibility, of which I am sure that a woman of your quality is incapable."

Crisson seemed to be having difficulty refraining from hurling himself upon Dove and strangling him, but he probably thought that it would only add fuel to the latter's criticism if he did.

Rachel, meanwhile, turned to me, as if to judge my reaction to

Dove's endorsement of my opinion that the wreckage of the machine ought to be buried at sea, as deeply as possible, but she saw as soon as she looked me full in the face that I was incapable of any reaction at all. There was no mirror in the room in which I could see my reflection, but Rachel's gazed told me clearly enough that my strenuous efforts to maintain an appearance of normality in spite of my hallucinations and my steadily-augmenting headache were no longer effective.

"David!" she exclaimed. "You're not well! Why didn't you say?"

"That was too much for Crisson, who was already at the end of his tether. He leapt to his feet and proclaimed: "It's a trick! We had a deal!"

Patterway, however, had come forward, with genuine concern on his face. "I'm as anxious to hear what Mr. Dearden has to say as you are, Crisson," he snapped, "but can't you see that the poor fellow is in genuine distress? Believe me, this is no trick."

He put one hand on my forehead and picked up my wrist with the other, intending to take my pulse. He blocked my view of Crisson, but not of Dove, whose reaction was even more interesting. He came forward too, just a eagerly as Patterway, almost elbowing the older man out of the way.

"What can you see, Dearden!" he demanded, urgently. "Tell me what you see! Damn it, man, you're in great danger!"

"I'm the closest thing there is here to a doctor!" Patterway snapped. "I'll be the judge of any danger he might be in."

Rachel was on her feet, full of alarm.

"It's just a migraine," I managed to croak. "I'll be all right. Just give me time."

"You need more than time, my friend," said Patterway. "You need sleep."

"No!" protested Crisson. "We had a deal! It's not fair!"

Dove had turned to Rachel. "I fear, Mrs. Tillinghast," he said, "that you might have made an error in asking Mr. Dearden to come back here. It seems to me that his exposure to your husband's radiation has had a lingering effect, amplified here because of similarly lingering effects of the house's long exposure. I doubt that you or the rest of us are in any danger, at least for the time being, but I fear that Mr. Dearden might be, He is, as you say, not well—not well at all. He needs to get out of the house, if possible."

"Nonsense!" snapped Patterway. "He certainly can't go gallivanting around in the dark on that appalling road, even if Crisson's willing to put his fancy automobile at his disposal, and the nearest hospital is more than ten miles away. We need to get the poor fellow into bed. If, as he says, it's just a migraine, he'll be fine in the morning. We can make another appointment—preferably in broad daylight—to hear his account of Tillinghast's death and…settle any further matters."

Dove was reluctant to agree, but accepted the strength of the argument regarding the impracticability of transporting me to another location. Perhaps, too, his curiosity to obtain an account of the effects from which he presumed me to be suffering was sufficient to counterbalance his concern for my welfare. "Very well," he said. "Will you help me to take him upstairs, Crisson, or are you just going to stand there seething?"

"I don't need any help," I insisted—or tried to insist. The words wouldn't come out of my mouth—not, at any rate, with the pronunciation I intended. They emerged as a complex combination of hisses and grunts. Thinking that actions speak louder than words, I stood up in order to demonstrate that I could walk unaided—at last, that's what I tried to do. It turned out that even standing up was now beyond my capabilities, let alone walking. My knees buckled. I tried to sit down again, but Dove had already caught me. He put one of my arms over his shoulder and Crisson, reluctantly, took the other.

Rachel, full of anxiety, led the way upstairs.

My two porters dumped me on my bed—rather unceremoniously, I thought. Then Patterway swept them aside in order to carry out yet another conspicuously inexpert parody of medical examination. He shooed Dove and Crisson away, and they went, as reluctantly as Crisson had come, bowing to the apparent medical authority, even though they knew that it was fake, so much did the weight of circumstance and ritual weigh upon them.

Rachel wasn't fooled, though. As soon as she could, she shoved Patterway outside too, and then ushered all thee of them downstairs, with the much more secure authority of a hostess under pressure. I heard her dickering with them, presumably about the timing of a further meeting tomorrow, and then I heard the door slam. A few seconds later she reappeared.

"It's not a trick, is it?" she said, just to make sure.

I shook my head. I was mortified. I felt that I had just ruined everything, that my knight in shining armor role had just turned to ridiculous farce, that I had shown myself up for the ridiculous weakling I was, and proved to her how right she had been to choose Tillinghast over me—for I was sure, now, that she really had made a choice, that even though I had not made any declaration, she had known that I was in love with her as well, and probably suspected that I still was. She had given me a chance to prove myself, and I had failed the test.

She sat down on the edge of the bed.

"Poor David," he said. "Dove's right—it's my fault. I dragged you back here, because of my own stupid selfishness. I hope you can forgive me—and I hope to Heaven that you're right, and that it's just a migraine, and it will clear up. I'd never forgive myself if….."

She left it at that. I had no idea what might have followed the "if," but I was convinced that my headache was just a migraine, and that it didn't matter.

I tried to tell her that, but the words wouldn't come out. I managed gestures, though, intended to convey he same meaning, and even managed to prop myself up on my elbow and nod my head. That might have been a mistake. The nod unleashed the full fury of the headache— but I resisted the pain. In fact, it even seemed to shake me up slightly. I managed to say: "I'll be all right." Then I pointed to my valise and pronounced the word: "Laudanum," very carefully.

She understood. She opened the valise, fond the clearly-labeled bottle, removed he stopper, and then ran out of the room to find a spoon. She didn't have to go downstairs to the kitchen; she was back in a trice.

I swallowed the dose she poured. Then I found that I was able to sit up, provided that I held my head very still. I loosened my cravat and removed it. Then, working slowly and meticulously, I began to unbutton my shirt.

"I'll be all right," I told her, heroically but incomprehensibly, and dutifully waited unto she had nodded her head to acknowledge the probability of the assertion before I collapsed again, cursing myself for my weakness and the universe for the bad timing that had inflicted the ordeal upon me at a moment when I desperately needed all my wits about me.

I didn't lose consciousness. Indeed, I was able to continue the process of removing my outer garments, with a little help from Rachel, and was able to insert myself into the bedclothes and lay my head on the pillow. Once I had assumed that seemingly normal position, Rachel seemed considerably reassured. I saw her glance at the chair beside the dressing table, presumably weighing up the possibility of positioning it by the beside and maintaining a vigil, like a nurse. I closed my eyes and pretended to fall to sleep.

I have no idea why I did that. I wasn't thinking clearly. Perhaps I ought to have been yearning for her to sit with me, to demonstrate her concern, to allow her to feel distress on my behalf, mingled with a little guilt for her part in my trouble. I suspect, however, that I was in no condition to formulate such a morally dubious scheme, and that I was dominated by my embarrassment at having let her down, showing myself up as a weak individual likely to break under stress, and not the kind of strong support for which she had asked, the kind of support that she needed.

In the event, after long hesitation, she took the decision to leave me to my apparent sleep, and went out quietly, closing the door.

6

The closure of that door had an ominous suggestion of fatality about it, but I tried to tell myself not to exaggerate its symbolism, that all was not lost, and that if Rachel were still capable of loving me, rather than merely having the innocent affection of an old friendship, a mere headache could not destroy that susceptibility.

Tomorrow, I tried to remind myself, in spite of the torture I was undergoing, *the confrontation with the three scholars will resume. I'll have my turn to reveal to them what I had already revealed to Rachel, and then, with the available information properly pooled, we can debate in a rational manner what ought to be done with the remains of the machine.*

Which way would that decision go? I couldn't tell. Given that Dove seemed to be on the side of destruction, that made two against two, the opposing two being deeply divided and unable to unite their efforts; in spite of Dove's overconfidence in his charm, I thought that there was every chance of persuading Rachel that destruction was the safer alternative.

On the other hand, perhaps perversely, I was no longer certain that destruction *was* the right option. Wasn't Patterway right, after all, to say that the possibilities of the new radiation ought to be studied, if possible, with care and discipline, by responsible scholars. In fact, although I did not like to admit it, what Crisson had said about the curious phenomenon of the susceptibility of two entirely different "genres" of radiation to form an alloy capable of mutating at least one of them was so very peculiar that it surely cried out for exploration and investigation. Was not Dove's simple equation of danger and the necessity of destruction too crude a way of thinking? Indeed, was not the fact that it had occurred automatically to a man like me further evidence of its crudity, its cowardice, and perhaps its stupidity?

There was no point in asking myself what Crawford Tillinghast would have done, as if I had often done in the past when confronted with enigmas seemingly beyond my own intellectual compass. I knew what Crawford Tillinghast would have done, because he had done it. And even though it had killed him, I was sure that he would have been horrified by the idea that his work might be destroyed.

I was sure, in fact, that if he had seen me taking aim at his machine, he would have stopped me from shooting it, even if he had to take the bullet himself in order to do that.

Did Rachel know that? Would she work it out? And if she did, would she do what the man she had never stopped loving would have wanted her to do, rather than what her improvised champion had advised her to do?

As that train on thought developed, it gradually seemed to become clearer and more coherent, and I realized that the laudanum was taking effect. The pain of the headache was easing considerably. The floaters did not disappear, but the opium dulled my sensitivity to their presence. They ceased to be alarming, or even inconvenient. I began to wonder why I had been so reluctant to have recourse to the drug, and why I was so wary of it. It was not as if it had ever done me any real harm; my previous experiences with its use had surely never been so frequent, so intense or so long-lasting as to create a serious anxiety that I might become addicted to it. I concluded that it must have been the fear of its possible hallucinatory effects that had deterred me—but as the headache eased, I felt more lucid and more in control of my thoughts than before.

I remembered that some of the European champions of opium-smoking alleged that the drug actually gave a clearer insight into the nature of things. The alcohol in which it was dissolved in the making of laudanum presumably did not help to maintain that lucidity, or that illusion of lucidity, but I was not a man to get drunk on a tablespoonful of eau-de-vie, so I felt entitled to assume that the opium had free rein to take effect—and it was certainly reckoning with the headache, which was a great relief.

I could still see the floaters, but I thought that I could see them more clearly now for what they really were: innocuous clouds, entities of mist, utterly incapable of doing any harm. How ridiculous it was, I thought, to be alarmed by the fact that they could pass through solid objects, including our bodies, since they clearly did not make any material contact in so doing, and could not possibly do any harm. Considered calmly and objectively, as I was now able to do, there was absolutely no reason to be afraid of them.

Tillinghast, obviously, had understood that, at least to begin with. He had insisted to all his correspondents that they were not hostile. He had viewed them with the eyes of a scientist, not a scaredy-cat. As he had told Patterway, he had set out to make a clinical study of their behavior, hoping to acquire an understanding of their nature and the habits of their existence. He had felt that there was no danger in that, or that, if there was, then it was a risk worth taking—and in spite of his flippant comment regarding ants and entomologists, he must have known that he could not pose any danger to them either, that he was in no danger of falling into the trap to which biologists are so prone, that the means of their observation affect the objects of their observation sufficiently to alter them, and sometimes to destroy them.

What, then, had changed? How had Tillinghast been reduced to the state in which I had found him, after a mere ten-week separation. How had he moved, psychologically, from calm and detached observation to a state perilously close to insanity, penetrated by terror and panic?

It seemed to me, in my restored condition of lucidity, that there were three overlapping possibilities.

First of all, obviously, there was the effect of the radiation that he was using. His focus of interest had been its specific effect on the pineal body deep within the brain, but it is a well-known truism of medicine that no treatment has only a single physiological effect. In addition to the intended effect there are always side-effects, some of which might be inconvenient, or even dangerous. The likelihood was that, as well as affecting his pineal body, Tillinghast's radiation had had other effects on the cells of his brain.

What were those effects? Was the terror he had felt—the terror that I too had glimpsed on the night of his death, and to which I had come close tonight before the kindly opium had restored my clairvoyance—a direct effect of the impure radiation, or was it a secondary effect corollary to the induced hallucinations? Perhaps a little of both—and if so, perhaps that dual effect had established a kind of feedback loop, by which the hallucination fed the terror and the terror fed the hallucination, causing a rapid crescendo effect.

Secondly, it seemed to me, at that point in my intellectual odyssey, there was the possible effect of Tillinghast's own psychology, which was a trifle paradoxical. He was a great scientist, a man capable of dispassionate and scrupulous observation and thought, but behind that methodological objectivity, there was passion, and a great deal of it. That passion showed in his occasional bursts of ill temper, often occasioned by rather trivial things, and it was manifest in the intensity of his feelings for Rachel, but it was also a significant component of his scientific endeavor—his "real passion," as Rachel had put it. Without the intensity of the passion that he had for scientific enquiry, he could not have contrived the stern and stubborn objectivity so necessary to accurate and fruitful observation.

Not all scientists are driven by that kind of passion, of course. Many, and perhaps the majority, are naturally dispassionate, calm and detached. Perhaps they are better equipped, psychologically, for the patient quotidian labor of science, but they are rarely the people who make the great breakthroughs, the leaps of genius. The work they do is invaluable, but it is rarely epoch-making. The passion of a scientist like Tillinghast can lead to great intellectual triumphs, but the popular cliché is not wrong in alleging that genius is akin to madness, and sometimes prone to achieve that metamorphosis. Perhaps ironically, it is most likely to achieve that metamorphosis at the exact moment of great discovery, the instant of conceptual breakthrough.

In that regard, Crawford Tillinghast might have been a psychological time-bomb, ticking away placidly while his research was in its early, routine phases, but ready to explode as the culmination of his efforts approached, increasingly vulnerable to some kind of trigger, perhaps as trivial as some of the triggers that could unleash his fits of temper—fits that Rachel and I had had abundant opportunity to witness, and whose cumulative war and tear had eventually proved too much for her, in spite of their mutual love.

Either of those two factors, I thought, or both in combination, might have been entirely adequate to explain Tillinghast's evident deterioration in the few weeks prior to his death, but the third possible factor could not be left out of account, in spite of—or perhaps because of—its awkward ambiguity. That factor was the actual content of what he had seen, or thought he had seen, beyond the strange parallel space in which the floaters lived, or at least existed.

In reconsidering the things that Tillinghast had said to me, or ranted at me, in the hours preceding his death, I could not get a clear picture of what he had seen, or thought he had seen, which had terrified him so much. Perhaps, of course, it was the terror that had produced the visions rather that the other way around, probably with the aid of a feedback effect that brought about a crescendo of terror and simultaneous hallucination, but the actual content of the hallucination still required examination and analysis.

It was at that point in the chain of logical analysis that Tillinghast's reasons for writing to Patterway and Dove, and what he had actually said to them, became important. Clearly, the sheer force of the visions had convinced him that he was dealing with something real, something capable of material effects—perhaps effects of the subtle order of the effects that the radiation was having in his pineal body and other parts of his brain, but nevertheless real. On the basis of his past reading, he had begun to link his own visions with other accounts recorded in the past, including those recorded in the Miskatonic documents and, it seemed from Dove's testimony, those in the archives of the Harmonic Society of Paris, an organization of occultists prey to the instinctive secrecy of such organizations.

What was the content of those visions? Dove had summed it up, apparently quoting Tillinghast, by calling them chimeras: beings fusing the loathsome aspects of various inferior orders of animals in hideous combination. That was, in a sense, only natural; that was the way that the human imagination worked in producing monsters, and in producing the very idea of monstrousness. It was a core element of the apparatus of mythology. Nor was it entirely a work of the imagination; everyone is familiar with stories of strange births, both human and animal, which they have seen in carnival freak shows and preserved in alcohol in medical museums, and everyone knows that such anomalous products of nature often seem to be hybridizations of one material species with another.

Superstition has long suspected, albeit without firm evidential support, that some such birth-deformities are psychologically induced by virtue of traumatic experiences during pregnancy. Pseudoscientific thinking has often suspected too, again without little reliable evidential support, that at least some mythical monsters are based on reports of actual creatures, which, although mistaken or exaggerated, nevertheless referred initially to real entities.

Patterway and Dove, evidently, were both prepared to accept the possibility of the physical reality of dimensions beyond the world revealed to us by the five human senses: not merely the atmospheric realm of the floaters but realms *beyond*, displaced in other spatial dimensions. They were both prepared to accept that such realms might be inhabited by living entities capable of interacting, in particular circumstances with vulgar matter, and, more pertinently, vulgar minds.

It was possible that they were wrong, and that the various entities described in the Miskatonic documents and the Harmonic Society archives were projections of the human imagination, products of the interaction of vision and terror, and the occasional crescendos and crises provoked by that interaction, and Occam's razor might favor that hypothesis…but it was also possible, was it not, that they were right?

Was that ambiguity resolvable? Probably not, I thought—but I had to try.

Given that I, unlike Patterway, Crisson and Dove had my own evidence to add to the pool, it was possible that I had a better opportunity, at least while the clarifying effects of the opium lasted and did not give way to its soporific effect, in seeing more clearly than them, and perhaps more clearly than poor Tillinghast, if I cared to make the effort, and if my probably-inferior intellect was up to the job. I felt that I had to try, all the more so as time might be pressing, because my present lucidity might not last.

Useful though the brief insights provided by Patterway, Crisson and Dove might be, they were far too lacking in detail to provide any strong guidance in the formulation of hypotheses. I had to go back to the one source I had that was prolific, detailed and intelligent, albeit far from consistent: the many philosophical conversations I had had over the years with Crawford Tillinghast. I strove to remember some of his more adventurous theses and analogies, as well as reviewing the elements of his cosmology.

According to Tillinghast, I recalled, there is no such thing as empty space or void, merely space whose fabric and contents are inaccessible to our senses: "dark substance," he called it, although he was at pains to assert that those terms were merely analogies, and only the restrictions of the language necessitated the use of such inadequate labels. The space between a man's eye and his outstretched hand, he was fond of saying, not only contains countless invisible and intangible entities such as the gases and vapors of the atmosphere and their multitudinous miscroscopic entries—inert dust particles, living bacilli, and so on—but also deformations in the spatial fabric that are far more complex than mere absence.

"We can have no idea of the complexity of those distortions," I remember him saying, once. "Perhaps they are mere wrinkles in the skin of our meager existence, but that is a very parsimonious supposition. Once we imagine a fourth special dimension, let alone a fifth or a sixth, the possibilities of what the universe might contain become literally endless. It is conceivable that the space that surrounds us—an, indeed, the space that is within us—is adjacent to billions, or trillions of parallel universes, which probably ought not to be imagined in a linear fashion akin to the pages of a book, neatly stacked and similar, but as entities possessed of all manner of shapes and sizes, entangled in unimaginably complex ways, some so tiny as to fit in labyrinthine fashion within the atoms of our universe and others so vast as to fit ours within one of their own atoms."

"And are there monsters there?" I had asked him, at the time, with what now came to seem suspiciously akin to a sinister premonition.

"In some of them, quite probably," he said, "but only those few sufficiently similar to ours to have imaginable contents. On the other hand there is no reason to assume any kind of hostility, even on the part of entities that might be horrible to the gaze."

At that point, he had been maintaining what Dove described as a "defiant optimism," but which he would doubtless have represented as scientific objectivity.

"But there is a blessing, is there not," I had persisted at the time, "in the fact that it is literally impossible for us to have any contact with any such hypothetical dimensions, because they are, by definition, inaccessible to our senses? Even if the monsters they contain are harmless...."

I remembered, then, something that had long slipped out of my memory, but which the laudanum—or the temporary combination of the laudanum with the hypersensitivity that was allowing me to perceive the floaters—now brought back to mind with startling clarity.

"No, no," he had said. "They are not inaccessible *by definition*. We do not know for sure what our senses might be capable of, or even how many we really have. The limitations of consciousness are partially deliberate and partially automatic. We see with our attention rather than our eyes, and what our memories remain is highly selective. The human brain might be capable of far more than the everyday uses than timid, tentative and fearful consciousness consents to make of it. Our ancestors lived in a world full of dire and mortal threats, when they had to concentrate their attention fully on the difficult business of everyday survival and the procurement of nourishment. But the world is different now, and our existential situation within it very different.

"Even very recently, only a tiny minority of men ever enjoyed a life of ease that permitted them the possibility of developing their intellect and beginning to the explore the possibilities of their visionary apparatus, but in the twentieth century, that minority has become very large, and in advanced political entities such as the United States, might soon constitute a majority. Many people will, of course, be quite uninterested in employing that leisure for anything but the pursuit of vulgar pleasure, but you and I, David, are cut from finer carnal cloth than that. We enjoy our pleasures, to be sure, and passionately, but we still seek, restlessly and equally passionately, for something beyond that: the knowledge of what our brains are really capable of achieving, if we can awaken and deploy their latent potential. The organ in question contains such mysteries—that of the pineal body, for instance...."

At that point, even my artificially enhanced memory began to fail in its exactitude, because the manner in which I had been listening to

Tillinghast speak at the time had suffered a distraction. Instead of following the course of his argument, I had focused on the use of his phrase "you and I, David," because I was far from certain that I was entitled to be included in that collective judgment. That what he was saying was true of himself, I had not the slightest doubt, but was it true of me? Was I really a seeker for something beyond the mundane, attempting to discover latent potentialities with myself?

I remembered, all too clearly, and painfully, that I had not only answered that question in the negative, but that I had wondered whether I could even qualify as one of the meager individuals employing my relative ease and freedom of thought for the pursuit of pleasure. Had I not given up that pursuit long ago—at the very moment, in fact, when I had felt compelled to renounce my ambition to seek happiness in marriage to Rachel—and lapsed into a curious kind of resignation and existential inertia, which had left me bogged down, incapable of moving in any direction toward any kind of personal fulfillment?

And, I thought, in looking back at that memory resurrected from the vaults of forgetfulness, was I not still there? Was I not still existentially becalmed, devoid of impetus. Was I still capable, assuming that I ever had been capable, of attempting to find some kind of fulfillment, of passionate amour, even with Rachel, to whom I had long ago appointed the position of the love of my life? Might I not have made that appointment, subconsciously, precisely because of the hopelessness of that love and the impossibility of its actualization? No matter what my consciousness thought, might I not be secretly terrified of the thought of actually having to make that love manifest, and practicable?

But that was not the point, I reminded myself, urgently. The point was the matter from which I had been distracted, back then and again now. The point was the pineal body and the other arcane mysteries of the brain and its latent potentials. The point was the possibility of a human connection with the dimensions beyond the wrinkled skin of the universe constructed by our senses, within the walls of consciousness. The point was the possibility of breaking through those walls, by means of opium, or some other chemical aid, or strange radiations, or some other physical aid. The point was: what, in fact, could the pineal body actually *do*, with the right stimulation?

I tried to focus on that, but it was becoming increasingly difficult. I could feel my drug assisted lucidity slipping away. Such states of mind never last. Opium, like scientific observation, is multiple in its effects. It never does just one thing. If it sometimes provides a marvelous impression of lucidity, it also produces other impressions, doubtless more useful to a mind in search of pleasant dreams and artificial paradises—which are often betrayed—but an inconvenience to seekers of insight, wisdom and conviction.

I tried hard to cling to the remnants of that lucidity even while I could feel it ebbing away, and knew that the ebb-tide was inexorable.

The pineal body, then.

Perhaps, I thought, I could actually invoke its support, and call its latent potential to my aid. Perhaps, on the other hand, it was already overactive, still suffering the lingering effects of the radiation leakage to which I had been subjected on the evening of Tillinghast's death. Perhaps I ought to be striving with all my mental might to force my pineal body to regain its erstwhile quietness.

I told myself, sternly, that it did not matter whether the body in question was presently functioning within my flesh as an organ of perception, or whether it was merely a source of illusory nightmares, or whether it really was, as Descartes had proposed, the true seat of the soul. The point was surely to calm its excitement, to reduce it to frigidity and indifference—as Tillinghast clearly had not been able to do. Surely, that was within my compass, even if it had not been within his, given the difference between us: he, the passionate scientist of genius; me, the....

But what was I, exactly? A schoolteacher, a communicator of orthodox knowledge in an orthodox manner, over a range of subjects that was broad, but which had, in my everyday dealings with them, little or no depth. Sometimes, the idea had come to me that I ought to have been the scientist and he ought to have been the schoolteacher, but that men are paradoxical creatures, whose vocations are not always in harmony with their temperaments.

That was foolish nonsense, of course, and even if I had taken a different course in life, I had certainly become a schoolteacher through and through, a creature of routine and repetition, of endless routine and endless repetition, like a hamster on an exercise wheel or a convict on a treadmill.

But was that not an advantage, now, when the residual stimulation of Tillinghast's radiation, reinforced by the leakage of the walls surrounding me and the creaking of that infernal weather-vane, was threatening to send my pineal body into overdrive? It was already enabling me to see the hidden inhabitants of the atmosphere, illuminating their dark substance; was it not only a matter of time before I began to perceive the dimensions beyond our space, and the monsters that inhabited those dimensions, the monsters that had disintegrated Gregory, Mrs. Updike and poor Jane…or perhaps only scared them into running as far away as they were able to go?

Was I not, precisely because of my lack of imagination, my intellectual inertia, better qualified than poor passionate Tillinghast, to fight the pineal furies of my enormously dull mind? Was I not capable of building walls around my consciousness far sturdier and more impregnable than his?

Except, of course, that I had been stirred by passion again. My long-latent love for Rachel, like my long-latent pineal body, had been provoked into action, into fervor, into desire, into hope....

But no, that was not a direction in which I ought to go. I had to concentrate on the pineal body itself, on the effects of its hyperactivity, which, whether they were real or merely hallucinatory, still had to be confronted, and fought, with all the intellectual weapons I could muster, while I armored myself as best I could with the chain-mail of intellectual discipline and the crested helm of rational thought.

Too colorful. Even metaphors might be dangerous. I had to try to be dull...except that, as a schoolteacher, such metaphors were part of my everyday apparatus, their color an invariable aid in trying to interest schoolboys, trying to make abstract ideas graspable, trying to equip those ideas to adhere to their fugitive minds....

The pineal body.

What was it doing? What might it yet do? The one thing I must not forget, although it had so far dodged my thinking, even while it had retained its seemingly full lucidity, was the reciprocity of its stimulated perception: the fact that, if that so-called gland really could and would allow me to catch glimpses of entities in the dimensions beyond, then it would also allow those entities to catch glimpses of me, and not merely of me but of the world to which I belonged, the macrocosm of which I was the microcosm, giving them and opportunity, if they really were the curious scientific minds that Patterway and Tillinghsat had wanted to believe, an opportunity for study, or, if they were the intrinsically hostile, quasi-demonic entities that Dove supposed, a point of attack, a means of exerting their hostility on me, and perhaps, through me, on my entire world, my entire reality....

But that was surely paranoia. That was surely nightmare....

But was not nightmare, now, where I was inevitably bound? Had not the soporific effect of the opium superseded its clarifying effect. Was I not asleep, having been asleep for some while? Was I not dreaming, only imagining that I was thinking clearly, only hallucinating the processes of logic?

Perhaps so. But on the other hand, no, I could not believe that I was *only* dreaming. I was convinced, and rightly so, that my mind, usually so adept at forgetting the idle produce of natural dreams, would not forget this one, even if I was, in fact, asleep. I was convinced—and, as I say, rightly so—that I would remember these thoughts in a far more vivid fashion than I remembered the routines and repetitions of quotidian reality. Whatever my brain was doing under the combined effects of the residual action of Tillinghast's machine and the tainted environment of the house, it was doing something striking, something that would remain with me, and not merely in memory.

It was changing me. I knew that, or at least felt it. But how was I changing? And what, exactly, was the "it" that was effecting the change.

And then I changed tack, as I remembered having done before, when my dreams became lucid, and seemed to acquire meaning. I tried with all my might to tell myself that I was only dreaming, that none of my fears were real, that when I woke up, it would be a new day, rich in bright late-summer sunlight, full of natural things, and real people: that Patterway, Crisson and Dove would return in order to complete our suspended bargain; that Rachel would be present, in the flesh....

But once again, no. That flesh, at least, was perhaps too dangerous an idea on which to linger. Better a more mundane, less stimulating reality than that, at least for the time being, when what I needed was a mental antidote to dreaming, not a wellspring of hope, ambition and... well, frankly, lust.

Routine and repetition. I had to be a schoolteacher again, at least for a little while.

And then the headache came back. Cosmic irony? Probably not. Probably just another reflection of the fact that the effects of opium are temporary, that they even have a backlash effect when they begin to wear off.

For a moment, I thought that the pain might help, as it had, albeit briefly, when it first became angrily insistent, opposing the dream, opposing the overactivity of the imagination, perhaps even allowing it to wake up.

It didn't help. Quite the contrary, in fact. As the pain increased again, it did begin to blot out the capacity for sequential conscious thought—and without the accompaniment of sequential conscious thought, perception becomes incoherent but not non-existent. Dreaming doesn't require sequential conscious thought; hallucination thrives on incoherence and inconsequentiality, and, of course, inanity and insanity.

Inanity and insanity were definitely not the effects for which I was striving, so I fought, yet again, to maintain my train of thought, and to keep it on the disciplined rails of stable consciousness, in spite of the pain and in spite of the various chemical effects of the laudanum. I wished, in a way, that perception itself had become non-existent, and, indeed, impossible, but far from it; however incoherent it becomes under pressure, perception remains, even in the absence of coherent consciousness, and is perhaps at its most dangerous then, when there is any danger in the offing. Such is the tyranny that three-dimensional perception exerts on conscious rationality, that when perception becomes incoherent, it becomes most ambitious in the direction of freedom, and when it becomes most ambitious for freedom, it renders itself at far greater risk of capture by the unknown, apprehension by the unapprehended, and hence at risk of injury.

I tried to concentrate, very hard, on the real, even though that is a very difficult thing to do when one is asleep and dreaming. I tried to focus on the disparate sounds of footfalls in various parts of the house, where it appeared that Rachel, Stephen and Emily were not yet in bed and asleep, although it seemed to me that the hour must be exceedingly late. Those sounds were too slight, and very possibly imaginary, so I tried to focus the creaking of the weather-vane, which was definitely real, although it had the disadvantage of always having seemed to me to be inimical, and it seemed even more sinister and insistent now that nightfall had freshened the sea-breeze.

I tried to capture the slight odor of dead fish that the breeze brought with it and insinuated through the cracks in the walls of the house, but that seemed a trifle nauseating, which was another effect I did not want. It seemed safer to concentrate on the tangible beating of my own heart and the susurrus of the blood in my arteries. That worked, to the extent that it could, but the pain continued to grow worse as the effect of laudanum continued to wear off, and the distortion of the dimensions became subversive, rebellious, anarchic....

I have no sympathy with people who describe their pain as "unbearable." If it were truly unbearable, it would kill them. Whatever we have survived was, *ipso facto*, bearable. There are times, however, when one cannot help but wonder whether one might, in fact, be on the point of dying—or, at least, on the point of fracture—when pain is hammering away inside one, especially inside one's head. All pain is, of course, felt within the brain, even when it seems to be coming from an ankle, a finger or the abdomen, but there is something about the self-referential experience that one's brain is actually *doing* the hurting that seems to add an extras twist to the agony....

But I mustn't go on. For one thing, there's nothing more to say.

Looking back objectively, and weighing them memory, all that really happened was that I had a headache—a migraine, in more pretentious terms. It probably lasted for an hour, perhaps two, or three if one counts the preparatory phase of optical and auditory phenomena. It calmed down under the effects of medication, got worse when the medication wore off, but then began to calm down again naturally, and gave permission to a deeper, more oblivious kind of sleep.

That was the long and short of it, in objective terms. It was bad, but it was manifestly not unbearable. In the beginning, there were strange impressions, odd ideas and occasional wild fancies, which I have recorded faithfully, but after a while there was only the returned pain, and after that, the bliss of genuine unconsciousness. Anything else I might add to the description I have just given can only be retrospective, hypothetical, and perhaps—of necessity—a little crazy.

The problem I have with sedatives, especially laudanum, is that one of their many side-effects is to enhance the craziness of subsequent reinterpretations of the experience. If laudanum numbs the pain—and it certainly does that, at least in the particular case of my migraines—that relief is compensated by the enhancement of the mind's obsession, the production of a kind of silent loquacity.

Given that the pain, when I woke up, was gone, and had been proven be the very fact waking up, to have been bearable, it seemed to me, once I had woken up again, early the following morning, that what I had to combat, above all else, was the potential craziness of reflection on the dream I had had, and could still remember with a vivid clarity that only comes from opium dreams, and rarely. It was, after all, the craziness that had killed Tillinghast. He had seen something in his own pineally-stimulated dreams beyond mere floaters, and presumably thought all kinds of thoughts beyond mere logic, and something infinitely more terrible in either case.

Perhaps, as my kindly ophthalmologist had suggested, and I tried firmly to believe, what Tillinghast had seen had merely been a by-product of his own particular personality, his idiosyncratic burden of common-or-garden accumulated guilt feelings…but what reassurance was there in that, really, even if I could convince myself that my own personality was less prolific in such by-products? Better to put all the craziness firmly out of mind, to polish my mental armor and strap on my rapier of reason, ready to do orthodox battle with the day, on my own behalf as well as my lady's.

Perhaps I was foolish. Perhaps, if I had really thought, with my waking consciousness, about the issues I had raised during my strange delirium, things would have worked out differently. But I didn't. When I woke up the next morning, glad to find myself completely well, with no trace of floaters in my field of vision, my one and only desire was to put it all out of my mind and make a fresh start. I didn't want to think about it—any of it—and I felt lucky to find myself in a state of mind, for once, where not wanting to think about it actually enabled me, for a while, not to do so.

On the other hand, perhaps that wasn't foolish at all, but exceedingly wise. Perhaps, I thought thereafter, if the craziness had got too solid a grip on me at that point, things would have worked out much worse than they actually did.

After all, I didn't die and I didn't go mad. Dove was wrong about that. I got close, and survived. I proved that, like pain, such things are, in the final analysis bearable.

When I woke up that morning, of course, I was overly optimistic. I quickly convinced myself, as I got out of bed, got dressed and washed myself, that if I could just keep my mind away from the unhealthy aspects of the matter, then I wouldn't see the same things that Tillinghast saw when he looked up—or, to be strictly accurate, in the direction *beyond up*. I convinced myself, too, that I wouldn't see something that was even more terrible *to me*, because I honestly thought that I didn't have the same capacity for terror that poor passionate Tillinghast had.

Perhaps it's odd, or a reflection of my stupidity, that I didn't return then to what might have been the most in question of all: the question of whether anything I might see would be merely an imaginary projection of my own private fears, or something real, reaching out from some dimension elsewhere in the plenum to capture me, and then perhaps to devour me, rip me apart, or compel me to undergo some kind of radical metamorphosis….which might, hypothetically speaking, be benign, but probably wouldn't.

7

I came downstairs at seven-thirty precisely. I wasn't completely recovered, as yet, but the pain had been reduced to the faintest of echoes, and I was confident that mere movement and conversation couldn't turn that particular tide and bring it flooding back. The floaters had almost entirely vanished, having faded to negligibility in a discreet manner that I couldn't help evaluating as tactful and delicate. It was almost as if the haunters of the house, if any remained from Tillinghast's unwise evocation, were now eager to hear what might come of the confrontation between Rachel and myself on the one hand, and our collective confrontation with the vultures or jackals on the other, and did not want any of the participants to be unduly inhibited.

When I appeared at the breakfast-table, the relief in Rachel's expression was palpable. Evidently, my face had recovered its normal composure, its old familiarity. She asked how I was feeling, of course, solicitously, but in the manner of someone who already knew the answer.

"I'm truly sorry," she said. "I had no idea that being here might have that effect in you."

"There's no need to apologize," I said. "You're not at fault in any way. I'm not at all sure that it was being here that brought on the attack—I've suffered plenty of similar ones at home, both before and after Tillinghast's death—and even if the location was the trigger of that one, the responsibility lies entirely within my own sensitive brain. I'm glad that you knew that you could call on my support when you thought you might need it—although I have to say that you handled your importunate visitors with admirable and consummate authority—and I'm glad that you did call upon me. I had a headache; it's gone now. I'm only sorry that it interrupted the process of settling things once and for all with the three jackals, and that we'll have to reconvene the colloquium. When did you ask them to come back?"

"Four o'clock this afternoon. I have other things to do first, and in any case, I wasn't sure how long you'd need to recover, or even whether we might have to take you to the hospital. I looked in on you two or there times during the night, though, and you seemed to be sleeping soundly. You weren't entirely serene at first—you seemed to be dreaming—but your condition didn't seem to be any cause for concern, and the last time I looked in you'd become much calmer."

"That was kind of you," I said. "You can't have got much sleep yourself."

"Enough," she assured me. "I probably wouldn't have slept soundly anyway, It's a little odd, coming back here after all these years. I don't believe what Dove said about the effects of Crawford's radiation machine but there are plenty of haunting memories here for me, of a perfectly ordinary kind. Do you feel up to confronting the unholy trinity again? You've already told me what you saw, so I'm perfectly capable of relaying it to them, if you'd prefer to return home."

"No," I said. "I'd far rather stay here, for as long as I might be useful to you. Of course I can tell my story, and it's far better that I do it myself, so that they can have the information directly from source, as it were, and in order to be able to answer any questions they might throw at me. Have you made any decision yet as to what you ought to do with the remains of the machine?"

"No," she said. "I was surprised by what Dove said, of course, in echoing your opinion—which I respect far more than his, of course—but I can't help feeling that there's a certain justice in Patterway's opinion, and that there's something criminal about obliterating any contribution to scientific knowledge, let alone Crawford's. When I ask myself what he would have wanted…what he, as I knew him, would have wanted… well, I think he'd have been utterly horrified by the thought that I might destroy his work, and I can't help feeling that he's never forgive me for doing that. In fact, I suspect that Crisson is right—that if Crawford had lived, he would have entered into collaboration with him, in order to recruit his technical expertise to the perfection of the machine. So, I'm still at sea, alas. I'm sorry if you think I'm horribly indecisive."

"Not at all," I assured her, in a true knightly manner. "I understand how difficult it is for you. I'm here to help, not to dictate. I gave you my opinion because you asked, but whatever you eventually decide, I'll support you fully."

"You're a good friend, David," she said. "But I'm afraid I might not be acting as a good friend to you if I ask you to stay here, even until this afternoon, let alone tonight."

"I want to stay," I assured her, with an honesty that I hoped was clearly manifest. "I want to see this through, and I want to be as much help to you as I possibly can."

"I won't be able to keep you company today, I fear. I have an appointment with the lawyer at nine, and then, depending on his ability to hasten the formalities, I'll have other things to do. At the very least I'll have to visit both the bank and the town hall. It would be optimistic to think that it will be possible to complete and file all the necessary paperwork in one day, so that all the bureaucratic wheels can be set in motion, but I want to get as much done as possible."

"I could come with you," I suggested.

"That's very kind, but I fear that it will be extremely tedious, and I'd feel easier in my own mind if I knew that you were resting and securing your recovery. To be completely honest, though, I'd rather you didn't stay in the house all day, just in case. The weather's fine, so it might be a good opportunity to take a leisurely stroll, perhaps down to the sea shore, and to have a quiet lunch overlooking the ocean."

I was surprised that she had organized my day for me in such detail, but her wish, however arbitrary, was my command. "I'll do that," I said.

"Good," she said, with apparent relief. "I hope to be back by three, and definitely by four. We'll have plenty to opportunity to chat for longer—all time in the world, once all the wretched formalities are out of the way. It will be much easier for me to make a reasoned decision about Crawford's things and my own future when the bureaucratic dust has settled."

That sounded promising to me: not merely the fact that Rachel wanted to have a longer conversation, but the implication that her own future would be one of the topics of discussion. By the time I had finished breakfast I was not only feeling fit and well but in a good mood.

Rachel set off in the car with Stephen to see the lawyer and begin settling the legal formalities attached to the execution of Tillinghast's will; I waved goodbye to her from the doorstep.

I wondered briefly whether it was safe to leave Emily alone in the house—not because of any evil effects that residual radiation might have but because the tea-chest in the attic containing the remains of the machine might attract thieves—but I dismissed the idea. The only one of the three predators who seemed to me to be sufficiently unscrupulous to hire a burglar was Crisson, and he still seemed confident that he would be able to buy the wreckage of the machine, the house and everything else. Rachel's instant dismissal of his offer had not modified that opinion; he simply thought of it as a maneuver in a bargaining process. The idea than anyone might actually be immune to the seductions of money was beyond the capacity of his imagination.

On reflection, in fact, it seemed to me that it would probably be wiser if I were not in the house, in case my presence there might attract visitors eager to anticipate the appointed time of four o'clock. If I were not there, Emily would simply be able to tell anyone who called that no one was home and send them away.

I therefore did exactly as Rachel had prescribed, and had a leisurely walk to the sea shore. Then I walked along the coast road for a while, and eventually found a pleasant waterfront restaurant where I could have a long lunch. The weather was a trifle cloudy, but very mild and pleasant; indeed, had it not been for the cloud and the breeze, it might have been uncomfortably hot. As Rachel has specified, I had a quiet lunch, gazing at the placid ocean, whose gentle waves seemed remarkably tranquil, and tranquilizing. I had recovered fully; I could not recall ever having felt healthier, or more optimistic.

I was drinking a cup of sweet tea after the meal, still gazing lazily out to sea, when my view was suddenly blocked by Lyman Dove, who sat down at my table without waiting for an invitation that I would not have given him. I looked around, but there was no sign of the other two.

"I'm sorry to intrude, Mr. Dearden," he lied, "but having spotted you, I felt obliged to come and ask how you were."

"Fine," I said, curtly. "It was just a headache. It won't happen again. We'll be able to conclude our business at four o'clock."

"I hope so," he said, chewing his lip pensively for a few moments before continuing. "You'll doubtless refuse to tell me your story in advance of that meeting, on the admirable principle of treating us all fairly, even though you find Crisson appalling and Patterway something of a crackpot. Nor would you tell me what Mrs. Tillinghast intends to do even if you knew, and if she knew, which she probably doesn't. Would you mind awfully, though, if I asked you a few questions about matters unrelated to our formal arrangement...?"

"Actually, I think I would mind," I told him.

He seemed disappointed, but not angry. "In that case," he said, "I'll stick to giving you information, at least for the moment. You surely can't have any objection to that, since you're as curious as anyone, and have a much bigger stake in this than I do."

For a moment, I thought that the stake to which he was referring was Rachel, but decided that he simply meant the alleged deleterious effects of Tillinghast's machine."

"I'm prepared to listen," I told him.

"Good. Let me say, first of all, that I don't believe you when you say that what happened to you yesterday was just a headache, and I don't believe that you believe it either. Even if it's true, though, I feel that I ought to warn you, in all seriousness, that if you stay in the house for much longer, you might be in real danger. I meant what I said last night about my research into these matters having convinced me that people who are driven by their passion for knowledge to investigate these things too closely almost always come out of it badly."

"Really?" I parried, making the interrogation point as weak as my tone could contrive.

"Yes. Tillinghast isn't the first person to conduct such an enquiry, and the radiation produced by his machine isn't the only means that people have found of stimulating the pineal body. Some have succeeded in doing so by means of sound—music and incantation, that is. Others have used drugs, while a few have contented themselves with pure meditation. Success rates have been variable and idiosyncratic, but once you combine the available data into a big picture, albeit a jigsaw with most of the pieces missing, the trend becomes clear."

"Thank you for the warning," I said, in a neutral tone. I paid the bill and got up to leave. Dove got up with me, and obviously had no intention of quitting me yet. I went down to the beach and began to walk along the sand in the direction from which I'd come—and in which, I presumed, he had followed me.

"From what I can judge," he continued, "most of the investigators, in Paris and elsewhere—including those at Miskatonic, of course—have always gone into the research with supreme confidence in their intellectual stability. Those who've glimpsed the darker possibilities have steeled themselves to behold or make contact with monsters, believing themselves to be capable of withstanding their presence. Very few of them, from what I can tell, have given as much consideration to the other side of the coin. You know what I mean, I presume?"

It was a challenge. I didn't want him to think me stupid, so I accepted it. "You mean that they didn't give as much consideration to the consequences of the inhabitants of other dimensions—if there really are any—beholding and making contact with them.

"Precisely. I presume that you've avoided giving too much thought to the question of what happened to Tillinghast's servants, whose disappearance might indeed have passed unheeded in many places and in the past—although here and now it has inevitably piqued the curiosity of the police. Their complete failure to find any evidence of their flight, and the fact that almost all their possessions were still in the house when they searched it following Tellinghast's death has, inevitably put into their narrow minds the idea of a murder. They've searched the land attached to the house looking for improvised graves, but their failure to find any hasn't deterred them from continuing to entertain the hypothesis. I, on the other hand, do not—not, at least, insofar as it points an accusing finger at Tillinghast. I believe that the servants were *taken*."

I did not have to ask by whom, but I could not resist the temptation to ask: "Why?"

"That," he said, "is a very intriguing question. There have been other such disappearances—and occasionally, if the recorded evidence is believable, the occasional return. Alas, no one appears to have been able to obtain much useful information from those who have returned, and everything they have said appears to have been dismissed by the unsympathetic as evidence of mere insanity. I would dearly like to have the opportunity to question such a person myself, but the opportunities are so rare…anyway, it's a great pity that the interdimensional kidnappers failed to take Tillinghast on the night of his death. He would undoubtedly have been better equipped to survive such an ordeal than the vast majority of people…better equipped than you, for instance."

Again, I rose to the bait and provided him with the prompt that he evidently wanted.

"You think I'm in danger of being…taken?"

"Perhaps not yet, Mr. Dearden, but I believe that if you spend much longer in the house, you might be. And the consequences of a failed attempt might be worse than success, as witness Tillinghast."

"Tillinghast died of a brain hemorrhage," I sad.

"Indeed. Do you know exactly where in the brain the hemorrhage occurred?"

"No."

"Nor do I. The official medical examiner, only concerned to establish cause of death, did not include that detail in his report, if he even bothered to ascertain it. But I can hazard a guess."

"Anyone can hazard a guess," I pointed out.

"Indeed—just as anyone can hazard a guess as to the motives of the abductors of the butler, the housekeeper and the cook. Tillinghast, I suspect, and Patterway too, would have placed scientific research at the top of their list, tacitly assuming that the stolen people might be subjected to scrupulous examination, experimentation, and perhaps even vivisection. People tend to judge others by themselves, even in the most extraordinary circumstance."

The worst imaginable fate for an ant, I thought, *would be to fall into the hands of an experimentally-minded entomologist.*

"But you disagree," I said, as an observation rather than a query.

"I do, because I think the philosophical assumption overambitious. I have yet to formulate a firm hypothesis of my own, and will refrain from doing so unless or until I can speak to someone who has first-hand experience, but I can think of several other possibilities. Doubtless you can too?"

Again, it was a challenge. I was resentful of being tested in that way, but my reluctance to appear to fail outweighed the reluctance to give in to subtle pressure. "Fishing for sport," I suggested, "given that I cannot believe that it's for food. Or, given that we are talking about something that is, properly speaking beyond the horizons of our imagination, perhaps some motive that we could not begin to comprehend."

"Indeed," said Dove, yet again. "I knew that you must have given the matter some thought."

I was uncomfortably aware that I hadn't, save in passing, because it had never occurred to me—unless I had repressed the idea—that I might be hooked by interdimensional fishermen, scientists or God alone knew what. Apparently, it had occurred to Lyman Dove, who really was trying to warn me of a danger—which did not necessarily mean, of course, that he was not a crackpot, or utterly mistaken.

"Did you take laudanum for your headache, Mr. Dearden?" he asked, suddenly.

"Yes I did," I admitted. "But I didn't see any visions—not the slightest glimpse of any chimera combining cephalopod, coelenterate and insectile characteristics."

"Very wise," he commented. I looked surprised, thus falling into the trap. "On their part, I mean," he added, "not yours."

I considered him for a few moments, and then said: "You're quite a humanitarian, Mr. Dove."

At last, I had caught him slightly off guard.

"Am I?" he queried.

"Of course. Surely you don't need me to explain?"

He thought furiously for ten seconds, and then guessed. "Because I recommended to Mrs. Tillinghast that she destroy the machine? Well, yes. Not only would I not want to expose myself to its dangers, but I wouldn't want to expose Patterway or Crisson either, in spite of the possibility that, were they to fall victim to their curiosity and then contrive to return, they might make better witnesses than you...but not much better, I suspect."

"I'll take that as an insult to them rather than a compliment to me," I said, dryly.

"The comparison is the same either way," he pointed out. "But yes, even though you meant your remark sarcastically, I am a humanitarian, to the extent that I would not want to expose anyone to risk of death, or perhaps worse, merely to satisfy my intellectual curiosity. I think even Crisson would draw the line at that. I won't pretend that I don't have a hidden agenda in talking to you, but I really am concerned that you might be in danger, and I would prefer you to escape it, if possible. I can understand that you're reluctant to abandon the hypothesis that all Tillinghast's machine did to him was to produce hallucinations, and that his own imagination did the rest, but someone who has read accounts of other events and collated the data, as Patterway and I have done, while not rejecting that hypothesis entirely, would feel obliged to take the other seriously. Many people insist on treating researchers of my stripe as lunatics, but I really don't believe that you can afford that luxury. If you wish, however, I shall abandon my attempts to persuade you and focus my attention henceforth on Mrs. Tillinghast."

That annoyed me. "What does that mean?" I snapped.

He looked surprised momentarily, and then realized why I had reacted in that way.

"Ah!" he said. "No, I have no intention on poaching on your romantic preserves. What I mean is that I shall attempt to persuade her that it might be dangerous for her to remain in the house for very long, especially if she intends to keep the debris of the machine there. You have every interest in supporting me in that, it seems. I shall stop short, however, of urging her to sell the house and its contents to Crisson, and persist in the more difficult course of advising her to throw the debris of the machine into the ocean, not too close to the shore, and then return to her village near New Bedford and put the Tillinghast house on the market. After a likely three month gap for a normal sale to be arranged, there should no longer be any significant danger to new tenants, so I don't consider it necessary actually to burn it down."

"For what it may be worth," I told him, "I've already urged Rachel not to stay in the house, but to return to her home in the environs of New Bedford instead."

"Ah," said Dove, again, albeit in a different tone. "Perhaps, then, we're closer in spirit than you want to confess. Good. We're allies, then?"

"On that point, certainly," I agreed.

"You must have known her for a long time?" Dove suggested, attempting to prompt confidences.

"Of course." I did not add anything further.

After a pause, he nodded. "Well then," he said, "I wish you both the very best of luck."

He sounded sincere. It was beginning to be difficult not to like him, at last a little bit, even though his supposed charm was largely imaginary. I had relaxed considerably since his silhouette had first spoiled by contemplation of the maternal ocean, and it occurred to me that his presence and eagerness to talk, however impolite they might be, ought to be reckoned an opportunity rather than a mere inconvenience.

"Is the Harmonic Society of Paris still active in occult research?" I asked him, by way of a tactful beginning.

"Oh yes. The golden days of Cagliostro, Mesmer and the Marquis de Puységur are long gone, obviously, and modern occultists like the neo-Martinists and the Theosophists consider the Harmonic Society quaintly old-fashioned, but it's by no means inactive in its investigations. The archives are still maintained, and the current custodian is working heroically to bring the catalogue up to date. I'm by no means the only scholar to have found the records of the members' explorations useful, and it has a fine library. Its manuscripts don't go back as far as those found in the Gobi and Yucatan, and the Antarctic artifacts held at Miskatonic belong to a much greater antiquity, but the Societé Harmonique has no reason to be ashamed."

I shook my head. We had come to a halt for no apparent reason, and I stirred the sand with my toe. "Have you ever heard of a village called Innsmouth?" I asked him.

"Of course," he said. "It has a certain notoriety in the circles in which I move. As a New England resident and specialist scholar, Patterway can undoubtedly tell you more about its legendry than I can, and offer you a biologist's perspective on the so-called Innsmouth look. He probably represents it in terms of mutation, although the term is rather vague and perhaps empty. You know more than you pretend, then, about my field…or Tillinghast did?"

"Tillinghast was interested in such matters," I admitted. "The prospect of metamorphoses, especially hereditary metamorphoses, intrigued him."

"As well it might. Yes, there are accounts of strange metamorphoses as well as death and insanity resulting from perception of the dimensions beyond space…or perception from the dimensions beyond space. I don't know whether Patterway holds to the thesis, but some biologists have certainly speculated that the pineal body plays a key role in embryological development, and that its capacity for orchestrating bodily transformation might go further than the repetitive processes of growth and sexual maturation, with the aid of the right stimulation. All earthly life is kindred, Mr. Dearden, and the metamorphic potential demonstrated by insects and amphibians might not be entirely lost to humans.

Organizing that potential might be extremely difficult, though, even if one has a means of stimulating the gland. Generating viable human chimeras is not something that can simply be left to random prodding. Had Tillinghast conducted any animal experiments with his radiation?"

"I don't believe so, but he might well have had plans to do so. Patterway didn't mention anything in his letters, but…."

"I agree. Patterway is one of those scrupulously honest men who doesn't always think it necessary to tell the whole truth, at least to begin with. If Tillinghast planned experiments of that kind, and mentioned them to Patterway, who thought it best to draw a veil over them in his account of the correspondence…well, it all adds up to one more reason to destroy the debris of the machine, don't you think?"

"We're probably worrying unreasonably," I muttered, although I really shouldn't have done so. "I've seen the wreckage and the surviving papers. The machine didn't just suffer a bullet-hole—it exploded violently—and there aren't any detailed plans of its design or construction."

"You'll never get Crisson to accept that. If Mrs. Tillinghast sells him the house, he'll probably tear it apart looking for a secret hiding-place."

"She won't. And even she did, there're isn't one. I knew Tillinghast—he wasn't a man for keeping secret hidey-holes."

"Men who do always make every effort to appear to be men who don't, even to their best friends," said Dove, with a sigh. "But you're probably right. In any case, I ought to leave you now—we're almost back to the path that leads to the Tillinghast house, and it wouldn't be a good idea for us to be seen together. Crisson and Patterway would surely cry foul, and that would add to a general animosity that's already too intense. But I'm very glad to have had this little chat, and I hope we'll have the opportunity to discuss such matters further. As I said, we appear to have more in common than you've so far been ready to admit. I hope that the migraines let you alone, at least for a few days, while you're still in this neck of the woods."

He didn't sound unduly hopeful about that possibility, but I assumed that he was just trying to frighten me. It wasn't necessary. I could have done that myself if I cared to think about it. I was trying not to. I had a duty to Rachel, and I intended to see it through to the end, whatever that turned out to be.

* * * *

I had only covered a mile of the distance separating me from the point where Dove had abandoned me and the house—I was approximately half way between the shore and the house, which was clearly visible on the hilltop—when Robert Crisson appeared in front of me, as abruptly as his competitor had.

He didn't bother to ask me how I was. "Don't worry, Mr. Dearden," he said, hastily. "I'm not trying to cheat by anticipating the four o'clock meeting. I just want to ask you one question: How much?"

"How much what?" I said, naively.

"Let's not prevaricate, Mr. Dearden. You're against me. I don't know why, but I'm not surprised. Lots of people take an immediate dislike to me. I have an unfortunate manner, I'm told. How much do you want to be *for* me, to help me get what I want? Name your price—conditional on results, obviously."

"You want me to try to persuade Mr. Tillinghast to sell you the house?"

"Yes. And to do anything else you can think of to get me the debris of the machine and the plans of its design. Whatever you can contrive. Whatever it takes."

His insolence took my breath away. "No," I said, simply.

"Why not?" he asked, bluntly.

I shrugged my shoulders. "Because the machine is too badly damaged to be reconstituted, and there are no plans. You're asking me to do the impossible. You're wasting your time, Mr. Crisson."

"Perhaps I am, but it's mine to waste." He hesitated, evidently feeling that a tactical shift was necessary, and then he said: "I owe you an apology, by the way."

Only one? I thought—but native politeness made me stick to: "Oh?"

"I shouldn't have accused you of playing a trick last night. When we got you upstairs, I realized that you weren't faking. It might well have been a delayed effect of the radiation, perhaps augmented by returning to the scene of the incident. But that's all the more reason why you should help me, isn't it? It would enable you to get out of the place quickly, and Mrs. Tillinghast too.

"Anyway, you've no reason not to help me. All you'd cost me by being stubborn is time. Now I know that the radiation exits, the hints that Tillinghast dropped in his letters will put me on the right path. Even if Mrs. Tillinghast does as that moron Dove suggests and throws the debris in the sea, it won't prevent the discovery being remade eventually—and if you really think that the debris will be no help in its reconstruction, you ought to be avid to help me. When I say conditional on results, I mean conditional on delivery of the fragments and the papers, not conditional on my success in building a new machine.

"I know that you're the key man in this, that the widow isn't going to reach a decision without asking your advice and guidance. You ought to set your antipathy to me aside, and think of it as doing her a favor. The offer for her house is the best she's ever going to get, and selling it won't deprive her of anything she needs. And if you think about it rationally, it will be obvious that you'll be doing yourself a favor too. So, name your price, and let's see if we can reach one that's acceptable to both of us."

"No," I said, again—and left it at that.

His eyes narrowed, as he tried to weigh me up. He thought that his arguments were sound and irrefutable. He couldn't understand my refusal.

"Pride," he said, finally, making a guess that wasn't far wrong. "It's said to come before a fall, you now."

"Actually," I said, "the Biblical quote is: 'pride goeth before destruction.' In the text, it's haughty manner that goes before a fall. I'll leave it to you to work out which of us requires that advice. Unless you were trying to threaten me?"

He shook his head. "I don't make threats," he said. "Waste of time. Bribes are another matter, usually. But you're frightened, although I can't understand why."

"Really?" I said. I was genuinely surprised that he couldn't understand why.

He shrugged his shoulders. "You think the machine is dangerous, because of what happened to Tillinghast. Well, perhaps it is—but I'll be the one taking the risk. I meant what I said about being certain that Tillinghast would have invited me to collaborate with him, in order that we could combine our expertise. He didn't know that he was going to be in mortal peril then, obviously, but he was a scientist. Wherever he saw potential dangers, he also saw potential rewards. A scientist doesn't turn away from unspecifiable dangers, as a man like Dove does automatically; a scientist's instinct is to face them, to triumph over them, and to claim the rewards of that triumph. So, even if reconstructing Tillinghast's machine might expose me to dangers, I'm not only willing but eager to confront them. I repeat: you have no reason not to help me."

I didn't want to concede the point. "You've made your position perfectly clear," I said. "I'll think about your offer."

He scowled. He was not a patient man. "Well, think about it, then," he said, ungraciously. "If you manage to reach a rational decision, just give me the nod at four o'clock."

And with that, he turned on his heel and stalked away, although I couldn't imagine that he was frightened that we might be seen together by Patterway or Dove, or intimidated by the fact that either of them might cry foul. Nor was he concerned that the animosity between him and his competitors might increase in tension.

I didn't meet Patterway in the course of the last mile. He was a gentleman, who played by the rules. He probably even believed, or pretended in polite conversation to believe, that cheats never prosper. I admired him for that, even though he was obviously wrong.

On the other hand, I thought, substituting the correct Biblical quote for Crisson's erroneous one didn't actually reduce the ominous quality of the alleged consequence of pride—far from it—and I was, after all, guilty as charged with regard to that particular sin.

The last half-mile to the Tillinghast house was steeply uphill, and I had walked quite a long way, so it was only to be expected that my tread would be heavier than it had been on the way down, but I felt weighed down by more than mere fatigue. Crisson had upset me slightly, and even Dove had made me feel uneasy. I no longer felt as well as I ever had, and although I couldn't see any floaters or feel any pain, I had the impression that the causes of my tendency to migraines were still nearby, and might come into play at any moment, once I was back in the haunted house.

8

Rachel was already back when I reached the house, shortly after three. The Model T was parked outside. I knew before I made my polite enquiry that things hadn't gone as smoothly as she'd hoped. There had been no nasty hitches, as such; it was just that everything was going to take longer than she had hoped, and far longer than would have been necessary in an efficiently organized world.

"I'll have to go back again tomorrow morning," she said, sadly. "Would you like a drink before we face the terrible three again?"

"Better not," I said. "I might need a clear head in order to tell my story coherently."

"Do you mind if I have one? Bureaucracy gets on my nerves."

"Of course not."

She poured herself a very moderate glass of bourbon. The chairs in the drawing-room were already set out in the appropriate number and conformation, in accordance with her tidy habits. We sat down together in the sofa.

"Are you feeling better now?" she inquired, solicitously.

"Much better," I assured her. It was still true, even though I had been deflated during my ascent from the placid shore. I wondered briefly whether I ought to tell her about my meetings with Dove and Crisson, but decided that there was no need.

"While I was in the car and hanging around in various waiting rooms in town," she told me, "I had another flick through Crawford's papers, but couldn't see anything that Crisson might find useful. You've seen the condition of the bits of the machine. I'm no expert judge, obviously but it seems to me that Crawford might well have taken his ultimate secret to the grave. Might it be worth showing the stuff to Patterway and Crisson while we're all together, in order to persuade them that there really is nothing worth squabbling over?"

"Perhaps," I said, cautiously. "From what I've seen, though, you won't convince Crisson. He's one of those people who can't let go once he gets an idea in his head. If you're really convinced that the material is completely useless, I suppose you might consider accepting his offer for the house. I don't know whether showing him the debris would put him off or increase his avidity, but it's a move worth considering. If you decide during the meeting that it's the right thing to do, it will only take me a couple of minutes to fetch the tea-chest down."

She nodded, by way of thanks. "But you still think I should throw it in the sea?" she queried.

I hesitated. "That's what my gut still suggests to me," I confirmed, "but it's not an objective observer, and you might not want to take its queasiness seriously. I do take your point about not wanting to destroy Crawford's legacy, and that's a much more serious and sensible argument than my vague unease. If you do decide that its preservation is your top priority, Patterway would surely be a more respectable custodian than Crisson. On the other hand, Crisson might be able to do more with it in practical terms, far more rapidly…although whether that ought to be an incentive or a disincentive, I honestly don't know…."

I felt that I was tying my argument in knots, and shut up.

"I'm not worried about money," Rachel said, pensively, although I had left money scrupulously unmentioned. "Like Crawford—and you, I dare say—I have enough for my needs, and I'm content with that, as you probably are." There was the briefest of pauses before she added: "*Are* you content, David?"

"With my income, yes," I said, although I didn't think that it was the state of my finances that had provoked her concern. The obvious exception implied by my reply was my state of health, and that was probably that had prompted her query—but I had far more in mind than that, whether she had or not.

It seemed that she had had detected my further preoccupation, or had been following a similar line of thought. "Why have you never married, David?" she asked.

"I never met the right woman," I replied, almost reflexively. I didn't meet her eyes. Had I not been uncomfortable anyway, I think I might have begun feeling distinctly nervous at the point—especially if I had met her eyes.

"Do you think you'll feel lonely," she asked, "now that Crawford's gone? You'd been fast friends for such a long time."

"I suppose I might," I admitted.

"Me too," she said. "It may seem absurd to say so, given that we were living apart and very rarely saw one another, but…."

"But knowing that he was there, somewhere within reach, made a difference," I finished for her. "I understand."

I thought I did understand. I also thought I knew enough about human nature to understand why there was a difference between continuing to love someone who was absent but alive, and continuing to have nostalgic loving feelings for someone who was dead.

"You're not too old," she said—meaning that I wasn't too old to find *the right woman*, to marry, to obtain a cure for loneliness, and perhaps to achieve the goal of true contentment. It wasn't an offer or a tentative feeler—not yet.

"I hope not," I said. "But I'd still need to find the right woman." This time, I did look at her directly, trying to meet her gaze as boldly and as suggestively as possible, but this time, she was the one looking away, evasively. My heart sank slightly, unable to think of that as anything but a bad sign.

"I'm sorry you fell ill yesterday," she said, deliberately changing the subject—another bad sign, I thought. "It might have been the octopus we had for dinner. Seafood can be untrustworthy, sometimes. The sea is said to be the mother of all life, but her cornucopia isn't entirely reliable."

There seemed to be a slight hint of bitterness in her voice. It suddenly occurred to me to wonder whether she and Tillinghast had ever tried to determine why it was that they had never had children, and what the doctor might have said to them by way of a tentative explanation, if they had made such a consultation. I wondered, too, whether a child might have prevented their separation, and made their relationship firmer. I thought that it probably would.

"It might have been partly the octopus," I agreed, "but I've been getting the migraines quite frequently of late, so there must be some kind of inherent flaw in my brain."

"Had the frequency increased before you were exposed to Crawford's radiation."

"Yes. The shock of his death might have been a factor in the most recent incidents, and the radiation too, I suppose, but it's a tendency I've always had, since I was a child."

"I knew you had occasional migraines, but I hadn't realized that it was such a stubborn and frequent problem."

I wondered how that realization might affect her opinion of me. It was difficult to dismiss the suspicion that it might work to my disadvantage

"It's not something I care to show off—unless, like last night, I can't help it. Then it becomes embarrassing. But it's under control I assure you."

"You've consulted a doctor, obviously?"

"More than one, and also a highly-regarded eye-specialist, because of the associated visual symptoms. They're still groping for an effective treatment, always suggesting laudanum as a last resort—but these things sometimes pass of their own accord." *And sometimes don't*, I didn't add.

"I'm sorry," she said.

Her sympathy was sincere, but there was a anxiety in her tone. Another bad sign, I thought.

You could simply tell her that you love her, and always have, I told myself. *It would be better than continuing to talk evasive rubbish about meeting the right woman and adding up quantities of bad and good signs.*

It was good advice, but I wasn't ready to take the plunge, and I doubt that I'd have taken it even if the doorbell hadn't rung.

We checked the clock. The terrible three were early.

I cursed them, obviously, but I knew that it hadn't made any real difference. I knew full well that I hadn't been about bite the bullet and let the cat out of the bag. I would simply have given myself the pretext that Rachel had already told me that there would be plenty of time for a longer chat when the business in hand was all done and dusted.

I cursed myself again, for thinking in clichés, although that was another regrettable tendency I'd had since childhood.

In the meantime, Emily had answered the door and showed the visitors in.

There were the customary formal greetings, polite handshakes and conventional offers of refreshment, but the vultures hastened through all of that, keen to get down to business.

It was my turn, and I did my duty with a reasonable degree of fluency, aided by the fact that I had already told the story once to Rachel. I didn't change it much, although I depersonalized it somewhat. All three of them seemed fascinated by my reports of what Tillinghast said during the hours immediately before his apoplexy, and I racked my brains trying to remember as many of his exact words as I could. They were even more interested in my description of what I had seen under the hallucinatory effects of the radiation.

Naturally, they had questions. Inevitably, Crisson was the first to barge in, with one that was rather more down-to-earth than those that his fellows were mulling over and still trying to formulate.

"Do you still have the revolver on you?" he asked.

I did. I took it out of my pocket and showed it to them.

"It's a small caliber," Crisson observed "It can't have done that much damage."

"It caused the machine to explode," I said. "Believe me, there was no shortage of damage."

"I'd like to see that for myself," Crisson said, and looked at the others, expecting them to back him up in pressing that request. They, however, were much slower off the mark, still thinking about what I'd told them.

"It seems to me," said Patterway, "that your account stops frustratingly short. You've given us a very clear account of the manner in which your visual perception of the space in the attic changed at first, filling up with semi-fluid entities. But if you've reported Tillinghast's words accurately, he told you to look over your left shoulder, because he wanted you to see something much more alarming—something he said, the mere sight of which made the servants scream before being, according to him, disintegrated. You didn't say, however, whether you did, in fact, look over your shoulder. Did you?"

The question was simple. The answer wasn't.

"I don't know," I said, honestly.

"You don't know?" echoed Crisson, scornfully.

"That's not fair, Crisson," Dove put in. "It's a perfectly honest and reasonable response. If Mr. Dearden did look, and did see whatever it was to which Tillighast was trying to draw his attention, it might well have been a perfectly rational stratagem for his mind to refuse to see it and his memory to refuse to record it."

"Only if you believe the kind of nonsense you do," Crisson retorted. "That stuff is all in the mind, all delusion and moral cowardice. On the other hand, perhaps Mr. Dearden ought to be congratulated on his lack of imagination. Whatever Tillinghast thought he saw, it certainly obliterated his scientific objectivity. If Mr. Dearden couldn't see anything at all, that surely ought to be regarded as a compliment to his presence of mind and sanity."

"But we don't know that he couldn't see anything at all," Patterway reminded him. "Even he doesn't know."

"Actually, Professor Patterway," Dove said, "Crisson does have a point. It might well be a compliment to Mr. Dearden's sanity that he can't remember what he saw, but there are two possible ways of interpreting that sane measure. It's possible, as Crisson seems to be assuming, that when Dearden looked round and upwards, he did indeed completely fail to see what Tillinghast was pointing at, and was reluctantly forced to conclude that his friend as delusional—in which case, sane politeness would insist that he take up a position of uncertainty, suspending his judgment of his own visual experience. On the other hand, if he *did* see what Tilinghast saw, then his protective sanity might simply have censored the image from his recoverable memory, in order to minimize its disturbing effect, imposing a benign forgetfulness. In that case, Mr. Dearden might well have retained the notion that he saw something, without being able to remember what it was. It would be unreasonable to expect him to be able to choose between those two alternatives, but it's not impossible that we might be able to do so, if…."

"Oh, this is all poppycock, and a complete waste of time," Crisson said. "This isn't a debating society, goddam it. The point is, what is Mrs. Tillinghast going to do with her husband's papers and the wreckage of his machine? She wanted to know what her husband told us about his research in order to help her make up her mind. We've done that. What I want to know is, when can I expect an answer to my offer?"

He looked directly at Rachel, throwing down the gauntlet.

As her champion, I thought that it was up to me to pick it up, so I was quick to interrupt. "Please remember, Mr. Crisson," I said, haughtily, "that Mrs. Tillinghast is recently bereaved. She has been kind enough, in response to your indelicately insistent enquiries, to compensate you for the information that you wanted from her by arranging matters so that you could have a first-hand account of the events leading up to her husband's death, but you must understand that all this has been very upsetting for her, and you really ought not to harass her. I'm willing to answer any questions you have, and even join in with speculative discussions, if necessary, but I feel obliged to demand that you give Mr. Tillinghast all the time she might require to make her own decisions in her own time. Should she want to make further arrangements with any of you, I'm sure that she'll contact you in due course."

I saw Patterway nod sympathetically, and Dove would probably have done likewise had he not been distracted by some train of thought that he was following independently. Crisson obviously wanted to react, but did not want to spoil his chances of success any more that his "unfortunate manner" already had. For the moment, he remained silent.

Rachel put her hand on my forearm and squeezed it slightly, by way of thanks. "Mr. Dearden is right," she said. "I'm not yet in a position to think clearly about all this. I'm sorry if I seem to you to be unreasonably slow, but I do need little more time. However…I think, on due reflection, that while you are all together, it might be as well to let you see the debris of the machine, so that you can judge for yourselves whether it might not be utterly useless and devoid of value." She turned to me. "Two minutes, you said, David?"

I didn't want to go. I didn't want to leave her alone with the three predators. I didn't want her to let go of my arm.

"Of course," I said, and ran up the two flights of stairs to the attic.

* * * *

I had to come down again at a more moderate pace, because the tea-chest was both heavy and unwieldy, but I made it in under two minutes.

I placed the crate on a side-table and returned to the sofa, gesturing with my left hand to invite the unholy trinity to feast their eyes on the unworthy objects of their optimistic desire.

Crisson and Patterway took turns to remove the larger fragments of Tillinghast's machine out of the tea-chest one by one, and they laid them out on the tabletop, with a reverence that seemed absurd for such small and shapeless items. Thy were careful, but I suspected that the dust that they were fishing out of the tea-chest along with the fragments, and spreading over the table, might well offend poor Emily even if they did not scratch the carefully polished surface.

All three of them contemplated the array, poring over the pieces, occasionally picking items up, passing them from hand to hand and turning them over. They even took politeness so far as to hand them on to their companions when they had scanned them. None bemoaned the parlous state of the fragments aloud, but the extent of their disappointment was obvious.

In the meantime, Rachel got up from the sofa and went to the bag that she had taken with her in her excursion earlier in the day. She removed a sheaf of paper from it and put the sheets on another table. Crisson was the first to reach them, but he did not attempt to hog them. He began to spread them out slowly and methodically, eventually forced to use the floor to display them, for lack of space on the tabletop.

The three of them took turns once again poring over the various documents on display, no more enthused than they had been by the shards of the machine.

Eventually, they got around to the inevitable question.

"Are you sure that there isn't anything more?" Patterway asked Rachel.

"Quite certain," she said. "There's nothing hidden away in some safe or secret drawer—my husband wasn't the kind of man to do that. So you can see now, Mr. Crisson, can you not, why it would not have been honest to accept your overly generous offer to buy the house and its contents?"

Crisson, as I had predicted, was not to be put off so easily. "To the untrained eye," he said, "the fragments might indeed seem utterly useless, but a careful census of the components, and some geometrical reconstruction in order to determine the fundamental features of their organization, might be invaluable in designing a similar machine. It will require meticulous work, but in the longer term, it might save me months, or years. The papers seem similarly unhelpful at first glance, but they're not devoid of information. My offer still stands, Mr. Tillinghast."

He glanced at me. I was careful not to nod my head in the slightest, lest he think it evidence of a secret agreement that I had no intention of making.

"Do you agree with that assessment, Professor Patterway?" I asked.

"I lack the competence to make an exert judgment," the biologist said, "but I have no real reason to doubt Mr. Crisson's optimistic judgment." He sounded a trifle deflated, apparently already resigned to the probability the Crisson would get his own way.

Dove was still turning over one of the shards of the machine, looking at it from various angles. He held it out to me, inviting me to take it. I didn't. He nodded his head, as if that proved something. Perhaps it did, but I saw no reason to rise to the challenge.

"Yes," he said, speaking directly to me, as if my stillness and silence had just made a cogent point. "I believe you might be right, Mr. Dearden. The machine is rather badly damaged, but I'm not sure that the pieces don't retain…..something. It's odd, and perhaps new. It's not something that comes up in the documents I've had a chance to examine, unless you count the musical instruments that some seekers have used in order to weaken or penetrate interdimensional barriers. There are definite suggestions that some of those instruments retained the effect of their usage long after the players put down their bows."

"Accursed violins?" said Crisson, contemptuously. He took the fragment that Dove was holding and weighed it in his right hand. "I can't feel anything, except the ragged edges," he said. "It's all in your head, man, can't you see that? You're frightening yourself with fancies, just as Tillinghast did—and him a man of science!"

Rachel had approached, and she took the fragment from him, to weigh it in her own more delicate hand.

After a few moments, she said: "I can't feel anything either. It's just a piece of…actually, what is that material into which the metal and glass components are fitted?"

"Bakelite," I told her. "It's relatively new, but it's very useful as an electric insulator, and it's also heat-resistant, so it helps to prevent valves from overheating, and I imagine that it has the same effect on the new tubes that produced Crawford's radiation. It's a kind of phenol formaldehyde resin—the near future will see the development of many such artificial organic compounds, I suspect."

Crisson looked at me in naked surprise.

"I'm a schoolteacher," I reminded him. "I'm not a specialist, but it's my job to try to keep abreast of current developments in household technology. I don't understand everything that Tillinghast told me, but I'm not an idiot."

"You've not only seen the tubes intact, then," Crisson said, "but Tillinghast explained their design and function to you—and you understood what he was telling you?"

I thought about that. No, I hadn't really understood Tilinghast's explanations; but yes, I had seen the tubes intact, and I did have a vague idea about their fundamental design and projected function. With a little expert prompting and a lot of mental effort, I might well be of some use in helping Crisson too construct a new machine...except that it was the last thing in the world I wanted to do, even for money."

"That's something that hadn't occurred to me...," Dove mused, frowning.

"You do surprise me," snapped Crisson, sarcastically, although I was sure that he had no more idea what Dove meant than I did.

The frown deepened, and Dove drew me to one side, anxiously.

"Don't worry," I said, in a low voice, "I'm not going to help him."

"I didn't suppose you were," he said. "Not the point. The situation—your situation—might be worse than I thought. You really do need to get out of here, Mr. Dearden, as soon as possible. And you really do need to have those fragments buried at sea—but not by your own hand; you were right just now to refuse to touch that one. But whatever happens, *Mrs. Tilllinghast must not sell those fragments and papers to Crisson.*"

I turned to look at Rachel, who was still holding the confused mess of bakelite, and copper, with the twisted stump of what looked like a perfectly innocuous vacuum tube of the Fleming variety, but was really something more complicated, and less innocuous.

I had no idea what she was going to do. I was certain that she hadn't made up her mind, and wouldn't, until she had talked to me at length and in earnest. But what was I going to advise, being caught between a gut feeling that urged me to agree with Dove on the one hand, and sane rationality on the other, in combination with recognition of Rachel's reluctance to destroy her husband's scientific legacy?

One step at a time, I thought. *Let's get rid of the vultures first, so that we can talk in private.*

That was easier said than done. My little dissertation on Bakelite had shifted Crisson's ideas slightly, although he was still clinging to the ones he already had, and had already broached.

"I owe you an apology, Mr. Dearden," he said—again underestimating the number. "I hadn't quite realized what a useful resource you might be, especially in view of the disappointing nature of these documents. Would you, perhaps, be interested in coming to work for me? I can offer you a much better salary than a schoolteacher's pay, and much more interesting work."

He didn't mention the earlier offer he'd made, of course, but that was tacitly included in the present one. I wouldn't be of any use to him if he didn't get the artifacts.

Everyone's eyes were suddenly fixed upon me, curiously.

"That's very kind of you, Mr. Crisson, "I said, "but I'm not really looking for a change of career. I'll think about your offer, obviously, and get back to you when I've weighed up all the pros and cons precisely, but I would advise you not to be overly optimistic."

Crisson seemed slightly puzzled, not knowing whether he ought to read that reply as a no, a maybe, or a bargaining tactic.

"It's possible, Mr. Dearden, that you might know more than you think," said Patterway, pensively, following the same line of thought as Crisson. "Not just about the machine, but about what happened on the evening of Tillinghast's tragic demise. At Miskatonic, my colleagues have obtained some useful results in recovering buried memories with the aid of hypnosis…."

"Good idea, Professor," opined Crisson.

"On the contrary," said Dove. "It's a very bad idea. Mr. Dearden might well have information that Dr. Tillinghast gave him, which has slipped his mind, and might be able to remember more of what he saw when the machine was set up in his presence and working. More significantly still, he might actually have seen something when Tillinghast instructed him to look over his left shoulder, which his mind has censored from his memory, for defensive reasons. Any attempt to recover relevant memories by hypnotic suggestion might release exactly what it is that his innate wisdom in trying to shield him from."

"Poppycock," repeated Crisson. "Mere delusion."

"Even if it were a delusion," Dove argued, "it might be no less dangerous…and not only to him."

Crisson shrugged. "My offer stands," he said. At least I had to give him full marks for consistency.

I would have been quite content to leave the matter there, but Rachel was looking at me, curiously and expectantly. Apparently, she too had not given any serious consideration to the possibility that I might know more about her husband's work that I had been able to tell her, without quite knowing what it was that I knew, as it were. It was for her that I felt I had to speak.

"I fear this is something of a red herring," I said, "I really don't remember how the components of the machine were configured, and I seriously doubt that Tillinghast said anything to me, in the course of the last few months of years, that would be of use to you, if I could somehow be induced to dredge it up from the silent depths of my memory. He treated me as Dr. Crisson did until a few minutes ago, and as any scientist would treat a high-school teacher obliged to operate across a range of subjects, however unfairly. He considered me to be an ignoramus incapable of understanding the words that he would normally have employed in communication with his fellow scientists, only able to follow the most rudimentary explanations couched in layman's terms. For that reason, he only made tokenistic attempt to explain what I watched him do. I'm sure that he went into greater detail regarding the fundamentals and direction of his research when writing to you, Dr. Crisson, than he ever did in talking to me."

Crisson and Patterway weren't satisfied with that. How could they be? They were both studying me, pensively. I suppose that was good, in a way, because it meant that Crisson was no longer attempting, for the moment, to exert pressure on Rachel, and she seemed glad to have that pressure taken off. She was looking at me gratefully, regarding me as her protective knight fulfilling my task, even though the shift in attention had been largely accidental on my part. I wondered whether I ought to encourage them rather than trying to put them off.

"Perhaps we can give you some useful guidance, Mr. Dearden even without the resource of hypnosis" Patterway suggested, stressing the *we*. "If Mr. Crisson and I can spell out the extent of our knowledge, much more fully than we were able to do last night, that in itself might be able to spark your memory, and allow you to get a better understanding of the machine's components and how it was constructed."

"Perhaps *I* can give you some such guidance," Crisson said, correcting the pronoun. "In collaboration, we might be able to fill in the gaps in your understanding and your memory. You and Mrs. Tillinghast really should think seriously about accepting my offers."

I glanced at Dove, but he merely looked back, knowing that I knew where he stood, and not feeling any need to reiterate it aloud.

Crisson evidently decided that more immediate prompting might be helpful. "As I understand it," he said, "Tillinghast had found a way to deploy electrical current in the generation of a new form of energy, fundamentally distinct from light, heat or Hertzian waves, although the side-effects of its generation included a visible glow that he described, a trifle awkwardly, as ultra-violet. Between the two of us, Mr. Dearden, I think we might be able to sophisticate your scientific understanding— which is, as you say, already greater than Tillinghast assumed—to the point where we could both acquire a comprehension of the design and functioning of his machine. I'm not entirely clear as to what detection and measuring devices he intended to use in order to register the presence and estimate the properties of this new energy, but...."

"I think I do," Dove put in.

Everyone looked at him curiously.

"We've all overlooked one element of the story that Dearden has just told us," Dove went on, "which is to say, the urgency with which Tillinghast begged him to come and see him, after an estrangement of some ten weeks occasioned by a petty quarrel."

"So what?" said Crisson.

"Mr. Dearden assumed, when he received the summons, that his friend was appealing for his help. He still thinks that. But Tillinghast might have had another reason. You wondered just now, Crisson, what devices Tillinghast intended to use to register the presence and estimate the properties of his new energy. Perhaps he had tried to do that already, three times, and wanted to try again. Perhaps Mr. Dearden was the detector, and the measuring device—or, to be more precise, the pineal body in his brain...."

Crisson became impatient again. "I really don't want to get into all your nonsense about sixth senses and other dimensions again, Dove. Essentially, this is a problem in physics—or, at least, the physics is prior to any question of application."

"Which is why," Patterway interjected, "the apparatus ought to be examined carefully and properly, in a university laboratory, rather than simply being handed over to Crisson so that he can *tinker* with it, and why Mr. Dearden ought to consider working with my team at Miskatonic rather than taking Crisson's bribe. Given that Tillinghast was evidently on the track of a fundamental scientific discovery, the matter needs expert and disciplined investigation by a proper scientific committee, not locking away in some modern alchemist's secret lair."

"Alchemist!" echoed Crisson, taking offense.

Partterway withdrew the insult with a vague gesture. "Merely a manner of speaking," he said, "much as everyone calls Edison a wizard.

"Turning this over to some sort of committee," Crisson objected, making the last word sound like a far deadlier insult than the one aimed at him, "would be equivalent to burying it for years on end. All of this"—his gesture included the fragments, the papers, and me—"requires energy and pragmatism. The point is to reproduce Tillinghast's new energy as soon as possible, then to explore its possible practical applications."

"Producing the radiation isn't the central issue," Patterway retorted, sounding slightly exasperated. "The point is to understand it. For all we know, the radiation might be all around us, in the same way that all sorts of electromagnetic radiation are around us, unapprehended by our senses and measuring devices—indeed, it almost certainly is, although Tillinghast's machine presumably intensified or focused it in some way. In the same way that Röntgen's discovery of X-rays depended on the accidental presence of a photogenic plate in a drawer to render their properties evident, however, what we need is some way of detecting, and thus paving the way to an analysis, of Tillinghast rays, or whatever they might end up being called. If Mr. Dove is right about the pineal body serving as a detector, and Mr. Dearden possibly having a special sensitivity to the radiation, it might be as well to study him carefully as well as the fragments of the machine...."

"Or not," Dove cut in, "given that's he's not a laboratory rat, and that any such investigation might do him irreparable harm."

The discussion seemed to be taking on an increasingly surreal tone, as well as an increasingly hostile manner. It was, I thought, enough to give anyone a headache...which was the last thing I wanted. Unfortunately, I was beginning to feel distinctly uneasy, although I couldn't see any floaters and my head wasn't aching. I simply felt peculiar. I became aware of the fact that I had been glancing upwards at intervals for some time. Looking for what? I had no idea. Why upwards? Why indeed?

"Flimflam," said Crisson, demonstrating that his vocabulary of insulting epithets stretched beyond *poppycock*. "What I'm interested in is what Dearden *saw*, before and during the night of Tillinghast's death—and I mean what he saw of the assembled and working machine, not hallucinations induced by the ranting of a madman."

"But that's the aspect of what he saw that's crucially important," Dove objected. "That's where the danger can be perceived, by those who aren't willfully blind. Whether or not the things that Tillinghast saw were or weren't mere hallucinations they still killed him. And if they weren't...."

Rachel wanted guidance. She gestured to the unholy trio, asking them to be quiet for a moment. "This is going too fast," she said. "Let's slow down. Please, David, can you help me out here. Did the radiation of Crawford's machine merely cause hallucinations, or did it really open up a portal to another dimension? Don't bother telling me that you don't know, because I know that—but what do you think, having heard these men arguing? I really need to know, in order to decide what to do with all of this."

Her "all of this," unlike Crisson's, was restricted to the shards and the documents, leaving me out.

What could I say? I didn't know—but I had to say something. She was relying on me. My feeling of unease seemed to be increasing, but it was unfamiliar unease, and that seemed paradoxically reassuring. It wasn't a migraine. I was in no danger of collapsing again. I felt strong and sharp—although it was odd, in that case, that I felt uneasy. What was wrong with me? It was still daylight outside, albeit slightly tired orange daylight, filtered by streaky cloud, and the illumination of the windows was perfectly adequate.

"Crawford's machine *did* cause hallucinations," I said, setting forth without really knowing where I might eventually arrive, "of that I'm sure. I don't pretend to know how, exactly, but I know that it did— and since hallucinations can be produced chemically, by opium and other compounds, I'm prepared to accept, in principle, that they might also be produced by some kind of radiation. Perhaps they are, routinely, when consciousness relaxes and we become vulnerable to dreams; perhaps all that opium and other chemical hallucinogens do is relax consciousness in such a way as to let ambient Tillinghast radiation take fuller effect. That isn't my province.

"Another thing I'm sure of, though, that that just because Tillinghast radiation produces hallucinations, that doesn't mean that it doesn't have other effects as well. I'm not sure that I can add much to the discussion that hadn't already been said, but for what it's worth. I've been carrying out my own retrospective investigation of what I saw, and I suppose there's no reason why I shouldn't share that with you."

I told them, then, what the ophthalmologist had told me about floaters and migraines, and how I'd extrapolated it to take account of what I had seen while Tillinghast's machine had been operative—and what *he* had seen, to the extent that he had communicated it to me.

"I might be wrong," I said, by way of conclusion, "But it seemed to me that the enhanced vision produced by Tillinghast's machine, at least with respect to the space that surrounds us, was perfectly real.

I'm beginning to think, now, that the semi-fluid entities that fill space, although they're normally invisible and intangible, really do exist, and part of the reason for that growing suspicion is that I've glimpsed them before, and thousands of other people have glimpsed them before, without thinking that they were anything more than everyday anomalies of eyesight. I suspect that I'm a little more sensitive than most because of my frequent migraines, and the specific preliminary symptoms associated with them, but I'm sure that other people can be found who are equally or even more sensitive. Perhaps the pineal body has something to do with it and perhaps not, but something is going on in my brain, which gives rise to periodic crises.

"For those crises, I take sometimes take laudanum, as a last resort. It works, but it has side-effects. There's no need for me to describe them in detail; plenty of other people have done that. The effects are assumed to be hallucinatory, because they clearly are, but it seems to me that there's also a sensory dimension involved: that opium really can, in the right circumstances, permit a kind of sight, which at least seems to extend beyond the three dimensions with which our minds usually equip space in order to make it imaginable and manageable. Are there monsters in that strange realm beyond space? Based on my nightmares, probably—but whether one can reliably base estimates of probability in nightmares, I don't know. We have to consider, however, that Crawford Tillinghast is dead and that three people have vanished without trace. The possibilities that Mr. Dove envisages can't be ignored—not by me, any longer, at any rate."

I had made that up as I went along. When I looked back on it, having finished, decided that it really was what I thought, at that moment in time, although I wasn't at all sure that it had been what I'd thought five minute before, let alone five weeks.

"Thank you, David," said Rachel, loyally. And then she looked up, uncertainly, as if she didn't know why she was doing it. She wasn't the only one, although that could have been an effect of suggestion.

"And that's why you shot the machine?" suggested Crisson, bitterly. There seemed to me to be an odd edge to his bitterness, as if he were steeling himself against some inner unease which he didn't want to become evident—just like me.

"I wasn't thinking entirely logically at the time," I admitted, "but now that I think back, more calmly, yes I think that's exactly why I shot the machine."

"How come you were carrying a gun, anyway?" Crisson demanded.

"I was robbed at gunpoint in East Providence last year," I told him. "It shook me up rather badly. I began carrying a gun because it restored something of my shattered sense of security. I still carry it. Anyway, I don't regret shooting the machine. The machine was dangerous, Tillinghast radiation is dangerous. If you succeed in replicating the machine and reproducing the radiation, it will be dangerous. Perhaps, if my nerves hadn't still been a little raw after the hold-up, I wouldn't have been so vulnerable to fear and I wouldn't have been able to react as I did.

"I don't know what caused Tillinghast's vulnerability, although it can't have helped that he'd probably been going without sleep for days on end. It can't have helped, either, that his servants had gone, however and wherever they went. Whatever the reason was, though, Tillinghast was utterly terrified that night, and we'd be fools to forget or ignore that. My one regret, looking back now, is that I didn't act sooner…much sooner.

"I don't regret the gunshot—only that it took me so long to fire it. If I had contrived simply to switch off the machine, or unplug it from the batteries, I dread to think what might have happened when Tillinghast activated it again—because he would have done so, even though he was terrified." I was speaking more rapidly than usual.

"Of course he would," said Patterway, pensively. "He was a scientist." Then he looked up.

"As you would yourself, James," said Crisson, "and I will, when I solve the mystery the Tillinghast left behind."

I sighed. There was nothing to be done with the two of them. But what of poor Rachel! Was she any nearer now in spite of all my efforts, to being able to make a decision? She was shifting nervously on the sofa, as if she were no longer able to find a comfortable place to sit.

"Do you have complete confidence in your own ability to resist terror, gentlemen?" Rachel asked all three of her guests, perhaps a trifle mischievously, although I had no doubt that the lightness of her tone was feigned.

"Although he was a scientist of distinction, Madame," said Patterway, pompously, trying to choose his words carefully, "your late husband did have slight tendency to…volatility. Not that there is anything wrong in a scientist having passion, of course, but firmness in objectivity is an invaluable asset, and…." He did not sound like a man possessed of firmness in objectivity, at least for the moment.

"And you believe that you have it in excess, Professor?" Dove interjected. "Perhaps you do—and before Mr. Crisson begins boasting on his account, I will agree that he certainly has a valuable dullness of feeling to compliment his natural energy and intellectual acuity…but I suspect that any ability to resist terror that you have at this moment in time might ebb away very quickly were terror actually to present itself. For myself, I'm wary of making the experiment. If that makes me a coward, so be it." He looked up, and I had the impression that he was more aware of the action than the others—and more anxious about what it might portend.

"We're still getting nowhere," said Crisson, fretfully "and it will soon be getting dark again. I'll accept, reluctantly, if I must, that neither Mrs. Tillinghast nor Mr. Dearden, are going to accept my offers immediately, but time is precious. Might I ask when I can expect an answer?"

I was tempted simply to say that mine was no, but I looked at Rachel, not wanting to speak before she did. She shook her head, but not to issue a refusal, merely to say that she was not yet in a position to make declaration of intent. She looked at me, still searching for support in her procrastination.

Because Rachel was looking at me, everyone else looked at me, as if expecting the judgment that I was so reluctant to make—and there was in their expressions something almost akin to desperation, as if they were criticizing my reluctance, blaming me for their own secret apprehension, for which they could find no evident cause.

But I could. Belatedly—perhaps very belatedly—I realized what was happening.

I was still determined not to let things get out of hand, to maintain the semblance of normality that suddenly seemed so precious. I met their silent censure as forthrightly as I could, and I actually opened my mouth, intending to say that perhaps we ought to adjourn for a second time, and meet again the following day—by which time, I hoped, clinging to that hope, that everything could still go on in the normal way Rachel might have been able to make her decision and the matter might indeed be settled in a natural and civilized fashion—but before I could make that thoroughly sensible and utterly hollow suggestion, I was interrupted.

9

Even the interruption seemed deliberately trivial, at first, and only prompted a more explicit contest against the uncanny. "Are you *sure* that noise is coming from the weather-vane, David?" Rachel put in, suddenly, and loudly. I had no idea why she said it. Perhaps she simply thought that moral support ought to be mutual, and that I might be in need of a certain relief. "Surely," she added, "we shouldn't be able to hear it all the way down here as loudly as we could in the attic."

I suspect that the three visitors hadn't paid any conscious attention to the creaking until then, dismissing it from consciousness as a mere trifle unworthy of concern—but when Rachel mentioned the word "weather-vane" all three of them looked up, reflexively, as if enlightenment were suddenly dawning and they had just realized why they had all been looking up repeatedly for the past half-hour.

They were grasping at straws. It hadn't been the weather-vane that had attracted their attention, unless they had construed its creaking as symbolic.

I didn't look up. I didn't need to. Instead, I said, matter-of-factly: "It's louder because the wind has increased in force since I went up to collect the tea-chest from the attic. Local breezes often generate turbulence as evening approaches and the sun's heat falls much more obliquely, because the land cools more rapidly than the sea, and…."

"You know, Dearden," said Dove, interrupting me with a cutting edge of anxiety in his voice, "I believe you were right about the canneries. I *can* detect an odor…."

"That's not the canneries," said Patterway, instantly, with a hint of panic in his tone. "I've lived in these parts all my life, and I know what the canneries smell like. That's the distant stink a dead whale washed up on the shore."

"No it's not," said Crisson, with an equal promptitude. "We're a full mile from the shore, and the breeze isn't that strong." He leapt to his feet, left the room and ran to the front door.

Movement suddenly seemed like a good idea. We all followed him, and watched him throw the door open.

"It's not coming in on the breeze at all," he said, then. "It's coming from somewhere in the house."

He stepped out on to the verandah and then leapt down the wooden steps, in order to look back at the house—*and up*.

Rachel made as if to follow him, but I grabbed her by the shoulders. The abruptness and force of the gesture made it seem that it was the first time I had made real physical contact with her, ever. I knew that coming outside hadn't made any difference. We didn't have to be inside the house to be under the spell—but I thought that it might be a bad idea for her to look up, just in case she caught a glimpse of what it was, without knowing it, that she was looking for.

"Don't," I said to her, urgently, impelled by my gut-feeling, which seemed suddenly intense. "Hold your nose, close your eyes, and try not to listen to that infernal weather-vane. Where are Stephen and Emily?"

"In the kitchen, I think."

"Good. Go and join them. Talk to them. Make sure they stay there. Leave this to me."

She looked at me in frank astonishment. "What is it?" she said, an edge in her voice because she didn't expect me to be able to answer.

"I don't know," I told her, "but it's *something*. Not a migraine, this time, for sure. I don't know how I know, but I know. I'm your knight in armor, remember. Perhaps the armor's rusty instead of shiny, but I have it. Trust me now, please."

Her blue-green eyes bored into me. Had I been on my own, I think she would have objected, perhaps even thought me mad—but Dove stepped forward, and said, rapidly: "Dearden's right, Mrs. Tillinghast. I felt it first when I was here yesterday afternoon—and I knew that he felt it too, although he was still in denial then. I knew that his migraine wasn't just a migraine, but I didn't know what it was. I still don't—but he's absolutely right. It's *something*, and it's getting a great deal closer, or at least more urgent."

Patterway and Crisson had turned to stare him uneasily. Crisson did not say *poppycock*, let alone *flimflam*. Whatever the something was, it had shaken him. What Dove had said to him a few minutes before about the possibility of his faith in his resistance to terror ebbing away once he was in the presence of terror must have suddenly taken on an ominous meaning in the back of his mind. He was by no means terrified yet, but he seemed to sense the imminent presence of terror, much closer at hand than a dead whale on the distant strand.

Rachel looked at me with an expression that I couldn't evaluate. "I want to stay with you," she said, flatly.

I wanted her to stay with me too, but I had a responsibility. I had to protect her, and I knew—I didn't just feel, but I *knew*—that she needed protection, and that the most dangerous place of all to be, right now, was by my side.

Something was coming, and I had a horribly nasty feeling that it was coming for *me*.

I took her hands in mine. For the first time in my life I realized the full import of Crisson's clichéd remark that time was precious. It hadn't seemed so only a few minutes before, when he'd trotted it out, but seemed starkly obvious now. The weather-vane was creaking, and there was a faint whiff of dead sea-life in the air, but they were only the merest of side-effects.

"I have to go up to the laboratory, Rachel," I told her, soberly. "That's where it is…will be. That's where it's coming to. You mustn't be there. Please, you mustn't. Crawford called me because he couldn't face it on his own, and I came. I came again, when you called, even though I knew, deep down, however much I didn't want to admit it, that I was going to have to face it again. I came to protect you, and that's what I have to do. Dove can come with me if he wants to, and Crisson and Patterway, if they're brave enough, but you mustn't. Go to the kitchen, please."

"No, Mrs. Tillinghast," said Dove. "Go to your car. Get out of here. As far away as possible." He looked at the Model T as he said it. Crisson's Cadillac wasn't blocking its exit, as it had been the previous evening; this time, he had walked from the hotel in company with his two competitors.

Rachel looked at Dove with an apparent contempt, but he wasn't deterred.

"Both of you ought to go," he added. "All of us, in fact. There's nothing Dearden or anyone can do. If he goes up to that attic, believe me, he's probably not going to come back down again."

Rachel looked at me.

"I can't get away from it...from them," I said, "if they really are coming to take me...but they're only *things*, not gods or demons. I don't have any alternative, but perhaps Dove's right. Get Stephen and Emily, and go, if you can. Take Dove with you...and the others, if there's room."

"No," she said, simply. "If you're staying, I'm staying. I won't go to the attic, if you don't want me to, but I'm not going to leave you alone in the house—and if he's any kind of a man, neither will he."

She meant Dove. She didn't even glance at Crisson and Patterway, tacitly ruling them irrelevant. I looked at them, though, trying to judge their response to the haunting that had suddenly descended upon the house, even though the sun hadn't yet touched the horizon in its descent toward the gray horizon of the land.

Crisson still couldn't muster a *poppycock*. He'd only been in the house for a matter of hours, in two separate stretches, and he hadn't felt a thing until now, but he'd been infected nevertheless, insidiously. He looked up again, and not at the creaky weather-vane. Then his gaze traveled downwards, over the property he'd tried to buy.

"I'm not going anywhere," he said, stubbornly. "If something's going to happen in the attic, I want to see it. No more stories: I want to *be there*."

All that Patterway said was: "Me too," but I knew what a depth of courage there was in those two words. Suddenly, it was becoming difficult to dislike any of them, even the appalling Crisson.

I glanced at Dove. "It's probably a once in a lifetime opportunity," he said, with a resigned sigh. "And it's what I'm here for, after all. I suppose I ought to be brave"

Rachel nodded in satisfaction, as if to confirm that it was indeed, what he and his companions were there for, as if it were for that reason, perhaps unknown to herself, that she had summoned them.

"I'll go to the kitchen," she said, meekly. "I'll help Emily prepare dinner."

She didn't tell me to do what I had to do. She didn't offer me any kind of token to suspend from my non-existent lance. She didn't give me a kiss. That was disappointing, in its way, but at least she was going to the kitchen in response to my request. That was enough. I only hoped that it would be enough to protect her from harm, if things went bad. But I knew, deep down, that it was me alone who had been glimpsed by monsters, while catching a glimpse of them. If they really were coming to get someone, it was probably me and me alone.

"Don't be afraid," I said to Rachel, hoping that the encouragement didn't sound as hollow as it felt.

"That's right," said Dove. "There are four of us, and not one of us is inconsiderable, as a scholar or a man. If anyone can face these things, the four of us can surely do it together…but they *are* coming, are they not, Dearden?"

I nodded my head, wanting to get on with it now—and whatever Rachel read in my face, she decided that there was no longer time for delay. She went back into the house: a courageous action in itself, in the circumstances.

Dove and I were only partly right, of course. Strictly speaking, nothing was *coming*, because it had been here all along, since long before the fatal night of Tillinghast's last experiment. It had been dormant for most of that time, but it had been *here*, or at least lurking in some vaster multidimensional space in which *here* was located, waiting for… what? A trigger? An invitation? A catalyst?

Waiting, I now suspected, ever since Tillinghast's death, for *me*.

I watched Rachel disappear. Behind me, I heard Crisson's voice asking of Patterway: "What do you make of that glow, James? What could cause a weather-vane to shine like that, even in the near-horizontal light of the setting sun, given that the glow is more purple than red?"

I heard Patterway reply, in a similarly intimate fashion: "It's not the vane itself, Bob—it's definitely some kind of reflection, but I can't make out whether it's coming from the sunset, or above or below, or…." He ran out of alternatives then.

I couldn't help it. I looked up. I saw the leakage of the purple glow, not merely shining on the weather-vane but illuminating the windows of the mansard from within, strangely and hypnotically. And I saw that the glow was getting brighter with every passing second.

That was when I remembered. Perhaps I should have remembered much earlier. Perhaps I should never have forgotten. Perhaps, on the other hand, the memory should have stayed buried a little longer, not emerging until the climax of the adventure, with a due sense of melodramatic propriety. Perhaps I had looked up reflexively and seen the glow with an utterly false tranquility, and brought my personal crisis forward.

At any rate, I remembered.

I remembered, abruptly, what I had seen—or to be strictly accurate, what I had *not* seen—when Crawford Tillinghast had told me to look over my left shoulder and upwards, at the thing or things that he thought were coming for him. Because I deduced now, even if I hadn't had time to do it at the time, that Tillinghast really had seen something out of his worst nightmares—in fact, something actually compounded out of his worst nightmares.

Tillinghast had seen some kind of loathsome chimera, reflecting— literally reflecting—his worst fears. He had seen a monster, the sight of which had pressed every trigger of his latent alarm, and had shocked the location within his brain that served as the organ of the mind's eyes, so rudely and profoundly that its blood vessels burst.

Crawford Tillinghast had seen his own personal vision of ultimate horror, and he couldn't take it. According to Dove, he was by no means the first—far from it. But I didn't see the same thing, nor my personal equivalent. I didn't see a nefandous chimera. I saw *nothing*…but not the comforting nothing that constitutes mere absence. I saw the ultimate nothing, the void that denies creation, the chaotic void that denies matter, presence and order, the limitless confusion that, for my perhaps-pedestrian mind, was more to be dreaded than any mere patchwork of slugs and cephalopods, spiders and worms.

Tillinghast had been a scientist, and a passionate scientist. He was a physicist, not a biologist, but he had still been focused on the material and the organization of the material, the world of atoms and molecules and structures, the realm of the active hand and the pineal body that might or might not be the seat of the soul—because, in Tillinghast's materialistic world-view, the soul did need a seat, something red and squishy, where it could sit, or sprawl, or wallow, or lie.

But I didn't think like that. I claim no credit for it—quite the reverse I suppose, because it really is symptomatic of a lack of energy and focus in my imagination. I saw primal chaos—which might not have been frightening at all, I suppose, if it hadn't been *coming for me.*

It wasn't like an active had reaching for me. It didn't have claws, or any kind of a grip. Had it reached me, it wouldn't have been able to take hold of me to carry me away, but it wouldn't have had to. Like a semi-fluid floater, it would have flowed into me, dissolving me from within, possessing me by disintegration. I felt sure—and I still feel sure that I had grounds for feeling sure at the time—that the dissolution would not be permanent or irreversible. I felt sure, on the night of Tillinghast's death, that I could have been reconstituted, elsewhere—having undergone a drastic metamorphosis, obviously, to adapt me or life in a different spatial plenum, but nevertheless, in some purely mental or spiritual sense, still myself.

Perhaps, had I been a different kind of person, albeit a very special one, I might have accepted that adventure. I might have been curious about what I might become, in a space unimaginable distant and different from my native space. According to Dove, some people had not only accepted the adventure, decisively or helplessly, but had actually come back from it.

Not me. When the monsters from the nth dimension, having glimpsed me in Tillinghast's attic by the uncertain ultraviolet light of his manufactured radiation, came to get me, I had ducked.

I claim no credit for that, either; it was just a reflex action of my own mind, probably—or at least perhaps—my pineal body. I had ducked, and that's when I lost consciousness, because I couldn't duck, in that fashion, in that circumstance, and stay conscious.

Perhaps, thereafter, I dreamed, and perhaps not. But in the split second before I ducked—the split second that was all I had before I had to duck—I saw, or rather didn't see, what it was that was coming for me, or what it wasn't.

I had forgotten it thereafter, presumably as a result of another mental reflex, some automatic tidier of the conscious mind, but I had remembered it again, after seeing Rachel vanish into what I hope was the safety of the kitchen, and then feeling the compulsion to look up.

I assumed, as anyone would, that I had remembered because I needed to remember. I assumed that I needed to know what it was that was coming for me. Why? I didn't know at the time, understandably, in view of the fact that my perception of the situation was still distorted, because I was still on the ground and not yet at the viewpoint where I needed to be, and where the something needed me to be, but perhaps my mental reflexes were cleverer than one might expect a mere reflex to be. Perhaps they knew that I would need to know, and perhaps they even had intuition enough to know why, although I certainly hadn't, at that point in time.

At any rate, I remembered.

I was tempted to tell the others—or Dove, at least, because I knew that he'd be interested, and that I might not have another chance to tell him.

But there wasn't time.

I shook myself, and pretended that I was shivering, although the evening was still warm. The twilight was turning gray, the sky losing its azure and the clouds their ruddy tint, but everything was lukewarm, even the breeze.

I turned to look at Crisson and Patterway. They were looking at me, waiting for a lead.

"Let's go," I said to them and to Dove. I was sure that an army wouldn't have been any better equipped to face them than one man, but I was glad I didn't have to go up there on my own. I didn't thank them, though. I knew they weren't doing it for me. They just wanted to watch me being swallowed up by the unknown, because it would be interesting. They were scholars, after all.

I wasn't. I was a knight. I had no arms or armor at all—no lance, no sword, no breastplate—but I didn't think that mattered. I didn't think that weapons of that vulgar sort could possibly make any difference to the conflict on which I was about to embark, against the primal chaos.

I was wrong—but how, in all honesty, could I possibly have known, or guessed?

* * * *

The stairs up to the attic were too narrow to allow us to go up four abreast, but not so narrow that we had to go up in single file. I was glad to have Dove by my side and Patterway and Crisson at my back. Suddenly, we were all friends, or at least allies, all ready to stand together, all needing to believe that we were capable of standing together. Dove was carrying a lantern.

I felt direly ungrateful, now, at having thought of my three companions so consistently as vultures, or jackals. At that juncture, I would far rather have felt that they were knights, like me: knights questing for a Holy Grail, who might actually be about to confront it, and might— please God—prove worthy, if not to touch it, at least to withstand its accusing glare, its merciless judgment.

I wanted them to be cool and collected too: mentally disciplined, immune to the passionate flaws that had made Tillinghast so vulnerable. I was confident of my own icy objectivity; I had to hope that they could match it, no matter what the monsters in the house—the monsters above and *beyond* the house—proved capable of doing, now that they had been further enabled by the sight of our world that Tillinghast's radiation had granted them. Doubtless Gregory, Mrs. Updike and Jane had played their part, as well as Tillinghast himself, and even me, in spite of the marginality of my role and involvement. As a cornucopia of human knowledge, the five of us left something to be desired, but still, we had been glimpsed, and distinguished sufficiently to generate the commencement of an understanding.

I knew now that it wasn't a matter of fishing for sport. I was confident that there was a higher purpose than that, or at least a more complex one.

I opened the door to the attic laboratory and stepped through, as if entering another world rather than another room. When all four of us were inside, able to stand in a line again, Crisson closed the door behind him.

I couldn't be sure whether the fear I could feel was mine or theirs, but I knew that I shouldn't let the fear feed itself, amplifying itself in a positive feedback loop. I had made that mistake before.

I didn't reach out to the electric light switch. There was no need. Dove was still carrying the lantern, but its yellow light had become irrelevant. The entire attic was glowing, with a beautiful purple light, much fuller and richer than the uneasy violet light cast by Tilinghast's machine, because it was a purer light. Obviously, its electromagnetic radiation was still alloyed with the other genre, but the combination was much more intimate now: a true marriage of fundamental forces.

There were no longer any shadows in the attic; everything there was clear—but the threat was not contained in shadows, because it did not need darkness in order to hide. The threat was in brightness, in the synthesized light. That was where it was hiding: in the cloak of imperious purple.

I knew all that, because I could see. For the first time, I could see clearly. The floaters that share our own universe, usually unseen, were still there, and still swarming, but they no longer caught the eyes. At least, they no longer caught mine; I think they were still confusing the others to a greater or lesser extent. The others had not yet undergone any metamorphosis under the influence of the radiation. The pineal bodies in their brains had not yet been stimulated by the radiation from beyond, as mine had, and although they were being stimulated now, the effects of that stimulation, if there were any, would not become manifest for days, if not weeks. But I had been present in the attic while Tillinghast's machine had been functioning, while something from beyond had been able to reach into out the space within my brain and perform an operation. I had hardly been aware of the resultant metamorphosis until I had first looked up to glimpse the purple glow, but my brain and its inner eye were now fully primed to respond to the new, pure light, and to obtain true enlightenment therefrom.

Mine was not the first operation that the *something* had attempted, but it was the first that had succeeded, the first to have reaped the fruit of groping practice. I was the first of its patients to have kept my sanity, my physical form, and my mental integrity…such mental integrity as I already had, at least, about which, I suppose, I might have had no reason to be unduly proud.

But I had survived, and I had been transformed, and now I could see. By means of the brightness, I could see through the floaters, the mansard and earthly materiality, into the further dimensions. I could see all the way through at least some of the further dimensions: those that were somehow intermediate between my own at the one from which the purple radiation was coming…because it was coming from a long, long way away, by a route that was in no sense straight, or even merely winding, but followed the contours of a Gordian knot whose inextricable thread ducked in and out of fourth and fifth spatial dimensions in search of the smoothest distance between two widely-separated universes.

"What *is* that?" Crisson whispered, referring to the source of the glow, looking up at the roof in front of the chimney-stack, where the base of the weather-vane must be.

"What are *those*?" asked Patterway, presumably referring to the floaters that were flocking around him, and moving through him, blinding him to the further realities, blocking his view of the further beyond.

Dove merely cursed, in stark distress. Perhaps he could see a little further than the other two, by virtue of the legacy of what he already knew, or the keenness of his curiosity, or simply a small random quirk of the structure of his brain. Perhaps it was that innate quirk, in fact, that had generated his fervent curiosity about occult matters, his quest for dangerous knowledge. He had known that it was dangerous, and had even had an inkling of why, but he had gone on anyway, like a moth drawn to a flame—and now he was here. Dove, I strongly suspected, could see the monsters beyond the floaters: the chimeras, the perverse summations of all that he found loathsome.

To give my three companions due credit, though, they all stood firm at first, and not because they didn't look up, because they did; not one of them kept his eyes on the floor. Not one of them had ducked as yet.

Dove dropped the lantern, and the candle inside it went out, but its glass didn't shatter. I don't think that a fire could have started even if it had, though, and the loss of its light was of no account at all. He didn't look down to see what had happened to the lantern, and neither did his companions. They all continued looking up, and none of them collapsed to the floor themselves, as many men in their situation would surely have done.

It seemed that Dove had the strength of mind and character to confront the worst terrors that his feeble, idiosyncratic brain could synthesize, for at least three seconds, perhaps five. The others held on a little longer than that, perhaps because their disciplined brains were more efficient censors, protecting them from the worst apprehensions of their imagination, or perhaps because they simply couldn't see as much.

For them, it was all hallucination. It was real, to the extent that it could have scared them to death, and real to the extent that the effects it had on their pineal gland might have imported the seeds of gradual mental, or even physical, mutations, and it was even real to the extent that they might have been disintegrated, and drawn into the labyrinth of that awesome Gordian knot, as Gregory, Mr. Updike and Jane undoubtedly had been—not malevolently, but clumsily—before the inhabitants of the nth dimension had got their hand in, so to speak. And because, for Crisson, Patterway and Dove, what they saw was primarily and quintessentially hallucination, they couldn't really *see*. They couldn't begin to understand.

Courage gave them time, but in the end, they had no other possible reactions but horror and terror, the latter following hot on the heels of the former. But they did hold out for a little while. They really were brave men, even if they did not pass the crucial trial by ordeal of perfect knights of sanity.

I, on the other hand, could see everything. I had been prepared. My pineal body had given me an enhanced perception on the evening of Tillinghast's death, and in perceiving, had been perceived, and in being perceived had established a feedback loop that allowed further enhancement. The crescendo had been slow, and might perhaps have died away if I had not come back to the house, which was still a focal point, by virtue of the force that had reached through the dimensions and whose interaction with the bullet I had fired had caused the machine to explode.

In the same way that Tillinghast's radiation was a compound of radiations of fundamentally different genres, the impact of my bullet had not been restricted to the simple material interactions of which bullets are normally capable. In the context of the alien matter, the matter of a different genre that was reaching into our dimensions, it had doubtless been a mere impurity, but everyone knows that even mere impurities can be deadly. In smashing Tillinghast's machine, that bullet had disrupted another material process, whose intended effects I have no way of calculating.

Calculation has never been my forte. But I could see, and thanks to the subtle metamorphosis that that I had undergone, when I looked up, my vision was not caught and trapped by the floaters, by the mansard roof, by the chimeras, or even by the appalling intricacies of the Gordian knot and all the alien universes through which its thread extended. I saw far, far *beyond up.*

I saw the machine.

I recognized it, even though it was bigger and more powerful than Tillinghast's machine. The technologists of the *n*th dimension, cleverer by far than Robert Crisson, had only needed a glimpse of Tillinghast's machine to grasp its fundamentals. That glimpse had not only permitted them to build one akin to it, but also to improve on it, to refine it.

Where, exactly, was the machine I saw?

In one sense, obviously, it was very far away, but in another, it was exceedingly close at hand. It had to be, in order to make the connection, and that was why the connection seemed so fiendishly complicated and entangled. The machine was unimaginably far away, but it was also close enough, quite literally, to touch. Even though it wasn't above us in the crude sense that it was overhead in our own three-dimensional space, it was weighing down upon us, threatening to crush us, or at the very least to crash through us, far more heavily and destructively than the impotent, hallucinatory floaters.

I saw it, and I think I remained calm. I think I did…. I suppose it's possible that I was actually terrified and panic-stricken, but somehow failed to notice it.

I can definitely remember saying, aloud, to Robert Crisson: "It seems you're not the only one who's been planning to duplicate Tillinghast's machine."

I think I remember that someone even replied, saying: "That's impossible," but it might have been Patterway rather than Crisson, and he might not have been replying to my remark at all, but merely making a comment on what he was seeing himself. I'm almost sure that neither of them could see the machine, because they were only looking up, and not beyond up. In any case, whoever spoke can only have meant that what he was seeing was "impossible" in the vulgar sense that it was just a hallucination. He didn't mean that what was actually happening, what was actually *there*, was "impossible" in the fuller sense that it was impossible that there was someone or something out in the wilderness of the manifold of parallel worlds clustered in and around the attic that had observed Tillinghast's experiments from afar—an *afar* of which Patterway had no conception—and had been far better able than any earthly mind would have been to understand it, to piece it together, and to set it in operation.

Clearly, that wasn't impossible at all. It was happening. It was real, if not-quite-yet-existent. And I could see it.

When I say "not-yet-quite-existent" I mean that when I first glimpsed the machine, it hadn't yet completed its metamorphosis from the primal chaos in which it had begun. The process of creation wasn't quite concluded. I could see that.

I felt no joy in that observation. Mostly, I just felt stupid. I accused myself of rampant egomania, for having thought that the monsters from the nth dimension, that evening, were coming for me, coming to capture me, and take me away. They weren't coming for me at all, any more than they had even been coming for Tillinghast on the night of his death.

That night, they had been coming for the machine—not the physical machine, which they probably wouldn't have been able to possess even by insinuating themselves within it, because it was inert and had no mental anchorage, but the *idea* of the machine, the specifications for the machine that were inside Tillinghast's mind. They hadn't tried to disintegrate him, to prepare him for metamorphosis. They had simply wanted to pick his brains. And they had. They hadn't killed him deliberately; it had been an accident—but they had killed him, crushing him from beyond above: *splat!* like a bug.

This time, obviously, it was different.

Tonight, they weren't coming *for* me; they had merely used me as a reference point, a bull's-eye at which to aim, in order to direct the beam of their radiation. I could have been anyone or anything. I was just something they were able to latch on to, because they had seen me before, and touched me before. They had seen me duck, without quite being able to get my head out of the way. I was convenient, but the choice, if there was any choice involved, had been entirely arbitrary.

I felt slightly insulted by that, although there was really no need, and it wasn't the important question anyway. The important question was: if they weren't coming for me, what were they coming for?

I don't know. I'm prepared to admit that. I don't know. But I'm also prepared to assert that it doesn't matter. They weren't fishing for sport, I knew that. Maybe they were, as Tillinghast or Patterway would have conjectured, scientists in search of knowledge, intent on studying our universe. Perhaps, as Dove would have dreaded, they really were malevolent, bent on destruction or perverse re-creation. I don't know. But I do know that whatever they actually intended to do, or try to do, the side-effects of what they did would probably have been catastrophic, not only for me, their reference point and target, and not only for everyone else in the house, including Rachel—the most precious thing in the universe—but perhaps Rhode Island, the Earth, or even the universe.

Whatever they were coming for, though, they would probably have attained it, if it hadn't been for one tiny flaw in their plan. I could see them. They hadn't changed me in order that I could see them; they had changed me in order that they could see me, so that they could use me as a reference point. But the process was reciprocal. In enabling themselves to get a fix on me, they had enabled me to get a fix on them.

They probably thought, if they thought at all, that it wouldn't matter. But they were wrong. They had chosen the wrong man to gift with that superlative sight. I saw what they were doing, and how. I saw the machine, and I knew that if its operation wasn't stopped, instantly, the results of its operation might well be catastrophic, not merely for me but...well, who can tell?

And that's why I did what I did, knowing, as I did it, what I was doing. I'm not going to claim ignorance, or that I acted by virtue of some uncontrollable reflex activated by panic. I did what I did deliberately, and I knew what I was doing, because I could see.

I'm not going to claim that anyone in my position would have done what I did. I know that Crawford Tillinghast wouldn't, for one, but I knew, too, that for once in my life I wasn't in a situation in which asking myself "What would Crawford Tillinghast do?" would provide an answer. Perhaps nobody else would have done what I did, if only for the simple reason that very few would have been able to do it—but it doesn't matter. I was there, I had the means, and I did it, knowingly and deliberately. The responsibility is mine.

I think I remember saying to my three companions, to Patterway and Crisson, at least: "Now's your chance." What I meant by that was that, real or illusory, the machine was there. All they had to do was look at it, if they could, and memorize its structure and design. But the remark was ironic, because I felt sure that they couldn't see it clearly through the floaters and the chimeras, and that even if they had been able to see it clearly, they were probably in no fit state to make disciplined observations and take notes.

I was really talking to myself, I think, because I was the one who had the chance, and the consequent responsibility. Even while the machine wasn't yet fully existent, I *knew*, in my hearts of hearts, or in the hidden depths of my brain, that I was about to see far more than I or any man had ever seen before: infinitely more than the split-second image of ultimate chaos that my pineal body had allowed me to perceive on the night of Tillinghast's death.

That was what I had remembered when I was outside, because it was all I had actually seen on that occasion, but there was more to that primal void even then than mere confusion, because in order to see it, I had had to peer through a whole series of subsidiary creations. I had only been aware of them as phantoms, but I had been aware of them. I might even have recognized some of them, if I'd been able to extend that split second a little further, because I had probably glimpsed them before, albeit exceedingly faintly, under the effect of laudanum.

Dove was right; Tillinghast's radiation was not the only means of stimulating the mind's eye, of enabling the dreaming mind to look beyond the consciousness of ordinary space—not deeply enough to become visible in turn to the farther populations, but a little further than here. On the night of Tillinghast's death, I had seen further than that—further beyond that—and that moment had been the fatal juncture in my life, but in my opium dreams, I had already gone further than my tiny, limited self.

I think I had known all along that I what I had seen before in my dreams was not *purely* hallucination, but consciousness is such a valiant shield, such a loving traitor, that I had actually contrived to talk myself out of knowing it, even while the new sight still lay dormant in me. I think I had known all along that Tillinghast had been at least half-right, or at least not completely deluded, and that his machine hadn't *simply* produced hallucinations, however monstrous, but really had made contact of a sort with the dark substance and dark energy making up the infinite leaves of the everpresent plenum…and I think I had known all along that once the pineal body had been altered—mutated or metamorphosed—in such a way as to recall its ancestral sensory functions, it couldn't possibly forget them again.

Some kinds of eyes can't be closed—but they can open further to let in *more light*.

Distantly, I heard Patterway—I think it was Patterway—start screaming. I heard someone else—Crisson, I presume—battering the closed door with his fists, unable to find the handle or to remember how to turn it. *So much for mechanical expertise,* I thought, unkindly. Most of all, however, I heard the screech of the whizzing weathervane, registering a storm unlike any that New England, or any other place on Earth, had ever experienced.

The attic was crowded by then, not with mere floaters, but with descending creatures coming from *beyond up*, which were undoubtedly solid, in their own frameworks of existence, but could only form phantoms in our narrow three-dimensional space, which was far too narrow to contain them. I saw jellyfish that were not jellyfish, cephalopods that were not cephalopods, and dead whales that were neither dead nor whales, although they surely stank to high heaven. I heard hisses that were not made by snakes, gurgles that were not made by fermentation in swamps or sewers, and screams that were probably not those of the damned in hell.

But they were all irrelevant to me. The only relevant thing to me was the machine, which was infinitely far away and yet close enough to touch. It was bigger than Tillinghast's machine, but not that much bigger—not the size of a barn door. The range was virtually point-blank, but I still had to take aim, with a steady hand. I could still have missed. And there was no shortage of potential distractions.

The chimerical monsters didn't bother me, because I knew that everything solid, liquid or vaporous, sharp, sticky or slimy, possessed of fangs, tentacles or glutinous maws, was mere hallucination. I could see beyond all that. I could sense whatever substitutes for hands were forging the replica of Tillinghast's machine out of whatever elements they had found to substitute for those of our tidy periodic table. I could see the entire mass of the dark substance constituting the unseen plenum, and the interplay of the dark energy that gave all the elements of the plenum activity, and light, and life. In a way, could see *everything*.

And in seeing everything, I could see how pathetically tiny, infinitely thin and direly tawdry our mere universe of stars really is, how forlorn the chasms between the stars are, how feeble the fires in the hearts of stars. That's what I mean by there being no shortage of distractions. The problem wasn't a matter of aiming the gun accurately, but of concentrating on the act of pulling the trigger.

That might have been difficult, under other circumstances, but not then and there, because I wasn't there for myself. I was there for Rachel, the woman I loved, and there was nothing tiny or tawdry about her, in my estimation. She meant the world to me. My concentration didn't waver, and nor did my hand.

Perhaps mercifully, there was nothing there to perform the function of a mirror. I couldn't see myself. I could see everything, *except myself*. I couldn't see that poor nondescript figure of rough-hewn flesh, that pathetic drop of bloody pulp with a small-caliber revolver in his hand. In my mind's eye, I was something much more grandiose than any mirror could have reflected, I was Rachel's knight, in glittering armor, wielding a magic sword: a sword capable of scything through the Gordian knot of the dimensions.

Perhaps it was merciful, too, that I was still carrying the gun—but how could a fearful mind like mine possibly have settled sufficiently, even after such a trivial shock as being robbed in East Providence, not to need that prop any longer, even in the intervals of experience when I was utterly convinced that I was a victim of hallucination?

Had I been a volatile man, or even a man capable of more than one passion, I dread to think what might have happened, but I am not. I am, fundamentally, a limited man, a man with a soul of unyielding granite, unbreakable even in the face of the unbearable. I have but one passion, and in its defense, I am a rock, a diamond, an intellectual paladin in icy armor.

Had I been in that attic as an adventurer, or even as scientist, I think I might have been doomed. I would almost certainly not have been able to fire that gun. And in that case, the machine that was being cleverly constructed somewhere in the further reaches of the multiverse by unhuman hands, from the raw materials of chaos, would not only have come fully into existence but would have remained, solidly establishing a bridge across infinity, a source of the light of creation itself. Patterway and Crisson would not have been able to lift a finger to oppose it, although they might have contrived to duck, once. Dove would surely have been destroyed or taken, simply because he was genuinely braver, or more determined in his curiosity. Had he been taken, I suspect that he might have been one of the few who came back—only, alas, to be considered hopelessly insane by well-meaning folk.

At any rate, it did not come to that.

What fools these immortals be, I remember thinking. *What fools, to use a man like me for a mere reference point, and to employ my presence in order to come here. They have no idea what a man like me is capable of doing, when his resolution is firm.*

In all fairness, though, neither had I—but I did it.

At the every moment when the newly-fabricated machine reached completion, when it achieved a kind of existence, here and elsewhere and everywhere in between…in that very split second, divided between a thousand intermediate universes, I took aim at the monstrous machine, and I fired.

I fired upwards.

There might be a pedantic sense, I suppose, in which I didn't fire at anything in the attic, because there was nothing actually in the attic at which to fire. The machine certainly existed, but it wasn't in the attic; there were certainly monsters in the attic, but they weren't substantial, and in any case, it wasn't them at which I was shooting. But I did take aim, at *something*, which *did* exist, however paradoxical that might seem in vulgar material terms. I took aim at what I could see, even though it was somewhere else entirely. I took aim, not with my dazzled, perhaps terrified material eyes, but with my other sight, the sight of my pineal eye.

In this three-dimensional universe, the tiny bullet followed a one-dimensional course, which took it between two of the roof-beams, enabling it to crash clean through the brittle roof-tile and its supporting felt, and then to hit the ancient weathervane—whose iron must have been exceedingly rusted and fatigued, because it shattered into tiny smithereens, as if it had exploded.

But the labyrinthine spaces through which the bullet passed, between our universe and the one in which it reached its true target, following a course that was not only not straight but more convoluted than the human mind can comprehend, were full. In normal circumstances, their fullness would have been utterly irrelevant to the flight of the bullet, because the substance and momentum of that tiny fragment of lead would not have been perceptible in any of the universes it traversed—but the circumstances were far from normal. The replica of Tillinghast's machine had been displaced from its point of origin in one of those other universes, extending throughout them all, physically, and in all those intermediate dimensions it existed, momentarily, as fully as it, or anything else, could exist. Furthermore, it had been activated.

If its activators had known what the effect of that extension and activation might be, how dangerous their operation was, would they have dared attempt it? Perhaps they would, if they were scientists, more passionate for discovery than safety.

However paradoxical it might seem, I didn't just fire the bullet in our universe. At any other moment of my life, with one possible exception, I couldn't have fired it in any other universe *but* this one, but at that particular moment, when the replica of Tillinghast's machine had opened not merely a gateway between the parallel worlds of the plenum, but an infinite series of gateways, that single bullet, or its ricochets, or the backwash of its passing, smashed through a whole series of universes—only a tiny fraction of those packed into the relevant space, in all likelihood, but trillions, of all sorts of shapes and sizes and convolutions.

In some, no doubt, the bullet or its effects would have been no more significant than a drifting particle of dust, but in others....

Size is relative, but size *matters*.

I could, and perhaps should, say that I didn't know what would happen, even though I could see perfectly clearly, with my mind's eye. I could at least take refuge in the assertion that I couldn't have been certain, but that would be a cowardice of which I'm not capable—for there are different kinds of cowardice, as well as different kinds of courage. Even if I couldn't have been certain, I certainly believed at the time, as I pulled the trigger and before the sound of the shot rang in my ears, and as my mind's eye followed the trajectory of the bullet, that I destroyed entire universes—not many, but a few.

I cannot be certain, but I believed at the time that I actually created one or two. I cannot be certain, but I believed at the time, that I precipitated metamorphoses in many others. Whoever or whatever had opened that catastrophic series of passageways through the multiverse, whoever or whatever it was that had created that uniquely privileged instant, that unparalleled opportunity, had allowed and caused me to wreak havoc on a literally unimaginable scale.

But I did not die and I was not taken. Nor were my three companions.

Patterway stopped screaming. By the time Crisson found the door handle, he no longer needed to open the door. Dove had stood firm— only for a matter of moments, obviously, but he had stood firm in spite of his terrors, and that speaks enormously to his credit.

I switched on the electric light, because the purple glow had vanished when the machine, provoked by my tiny bullet, exploded.

Can I say that I saved the lives of Patterway, Crisson and Dove? Probably. Perhaps all they would have had to do was duck, but they might not have managed it in time. And in any case, they did not have to. Yes, I saved their lives, and perhaps many more, including Rachel's. I protected everyone who would have been in danger. And I certainly believed then, and still believe, that everyone in the house, and perhaps much further afield, needed that protection.

What might have happened to Rachel, to Providence, to the United States, to the world, if I had not fired that shot? Who can tell? Perhaps nothing. Perhaps anything. But I knew, as soon as I had fired it, and as soon as I had seen the alien machine explode by virtue of the tension of the complex forces involved in its construction, that it was finished, that the sequence of bridges and gateways could not be reconnected. I was confident that even if Crisson were to succeed, some day, in reconstructing a machine similar to Tillinghast's, it would not prompt the inhabitants of the nth dimension to attempt to make fruitful contact with ours again.

Once bitten, as the cliché has it, twice shy.

10

Might I have held my fire, if I had realized more fully beforehand what the effects of the shot would be? Should I have fired anyway, on the grounds that the right to defend oneself, one's house, one friends, one's world or one's universe is absolute? Or should I have held my fire, thinking that the principle of the greatest good of the greatest number required me to take the risk of sacrificing myself, my friends, or my world, in order to spare all the other beings that surely died as my bullet followed its horrid trajectory?

Many of the beings that died, of course, must have been monsters from our point of view, chimerical creatures reflective of our worst nightmares. But that judgment is reciprocal. From their viewpoint, humans might well be utterly repulsive, nauseating, and unthinkable, and so far as they were concerned it was exactly such a nightmare creature, such a demon from the utmost depths of Hell, that had wreaked havoc and destruction in their worlds.

Perhaps, therefore, I should have held my fire. I don't even know, for sure, what might have happened to our world if I hadn't fired that shot so rapidly, or had my aim not been as true. Maybe nothing, beyond the confines of Rachel Tillinghast's house. Maybe, in fact, the intentions of the duplicators of Tillinghast's machine really were benign, even if their methods were scary. Maybe they had no intention of destruction, and maybe any metamorphosis they wrought, accidentally or deliberately would have been innocuous in its consequences. I don't know. But I know that I was mortally afraid. I know that that I was secretly terrified. I know that when I saw *everything*, in spite of the superficial coolness of my mind and my indomitable indifference, I was secretly overwhelmed by such an appalling cosmic horror that I wasn't at all sure that I could return from that existential brink alive, or sane. But I held my nerve.

I *have* returned, obviously. I'm alive. Am I sane? I think so, but it's said that many madmen think that, so perhaps I ought to reserve judgment. From the viewpoint of other people to whom I've told the story, it seems like nothing but a catalogue of delusions, a matter of pure hallucination. I know it wasn't, but I don't have any material proof, and the evidence of the three witnesses, even Lyman Dove's, hasn't lent me any substantial support.

So, all in all, perhaps I am mad. Perhaps it was all delusion. This written account probably won't suffice to convince anyone that I'm not.

Only I know the truth. Only I can.

In the attic, once the echoes had died away, it was my turn to say to my companions: "Are you all right?"

"Apparently," was Dove's dry response.

"Yes," said Crisson, curtly.

"No," Patterway replied. "That is, perhaps. I seem to have survived physically unscathed…but is it ever possible to say that one has survived an experience like that *unscathed*."

"There was a machine here," said Crisson. "I saw it, momentarily. I can even remember you telling me that my chance had come to study it. Where is it?"

"Gone," I said.

"Gone where?"

"Exploded."

"You mean that you shot the damn thing *again?*" He seemed horrified. He was once again in a condition to he horrified by things like that.

"Yes."

"Then where are the pieces?"

"Not here. It was only here for a fraction of a second. The bullet didn't hit it here. It hit it…somewhere else. That's where the pieces are."

"Damnation," he said.

"There's no damnation about it," Dove told him. "We had a narrow escape. I, for one, am very glad you had that gun, Dearden, and whatever you shot at, I'm very glad that you hit it."

"You didn't see it?"

"I saw the monsters—far more than I expected to see—but no, I didn't see any machine, and if it was one of the monsters you hit, I didn't see which one."

"I saw the monsters too," muttered Patterway. "Now I understand the Miskatonic documents." He turned to Crisson. "Don't say you didn't see them, Crisson."

"There was a machine," Crisson repeated, stubbornly. "It was only visible for a moment, but there was definitely a machine like Tillinghast's, which created hallucinations, like Tillinghast's. I was by the door, trying to get it open, but I looked over my shoulder. The machine was…*up there*." He pointed at the hole in the roof.

"You didn't see the monsters?" Dove asked him, interested.

"Yes, I saw monsters, but they weren't real. You can see for yourself that they've vanished into thin air. All it needed was a *bang* from a small-caliber revolver."

All it needed! I thought. *If only he knew!*

I didn't tell him. What would have been the point?

"Well," I said, after a decent interval, "if you're all fit and well, we'd better go downstairs to reassure Rachel. She'll be worried about us."

I thought the *us* was generous, but perhaps not unduly so.

We went back downstairs. Rachel had, indeed, been worried about us, although the worry had diminished when she had realized that the haunting presence weighing upon the house had been dissipated.

"I heard a gunshot," she said.

"Yes," I said. "It seemed to do the trick. "There's a hole in your roof, though, and the weather-vane shattered. You might have to give Mr. Crisson a slight discount if you decide to sell the house, and if he still wants to buy it."

The word *buy* seemed to galvanize the man of business doubling as a scientist. "The offer still stands," he said, stubbornly.

"Tomorrow," said Rachel, "I'll give you an answer tomorrow. Four o'clock."

Crisson didn't argue. He went to find his hat, and then took his leave.

It was pitch dark outside. "I'll walk with you," Patterway was quick to say.

"Me too, if I may," Dove put in.

None of them wanted to walk through the night alone. They all left together.

I had gone to sit down on the drawing room sofa, but Rachel invited me into the dining room. Dinner was about to be served.

She sat down opposite me, and said: "Well?"

I told her the whole story, without leaving out any detail that I could remember, but without the more colorful embellishments of my thought processes. I stuck to the facts, so far as I could judge them, and didn't sugar-coat them. On the other hand, I did tell her that I honestly believed that firing that shot had saved my life, and the lives of my companions, and perhaps also her life and the lives of her servants. I didn't add the entire human race, because that would have seemed to be exaggeration even to me. Obviously, I didn't tell her that I'd done it all for her, and no one else, and that if I hadn't been doing it for her, I wouldn't have been able to do it at all—but I did include saving her, tacitly, on the side of my moral credit.

"Of course," I added, scrupulously, at the end, because I could see the expression on her face, "it might have been a hallucination. I can't prove otherwise."

"Just a hallucination?" she asked, skeptically.

"Or unjust. I haven't quite made up my mind about that. But the light was real. You saw the light."

"I heard the screams too," she said. "But not you—you didn't scream.

"No," I said. "I didn't.

"Even if it was just a hallucination," she said, after a minute's thought, "you did what you had to do, and it appears that it worked. Will they come back, do you think?"

"My impression was that they won't, but I can't offer any guarantees."

"Do you still think I ought to throw the remains of the machine into the sea?"

I hesitated, but eventually, I said: "Not necessarily. Crawford deserves his legacy, and I think it's safe now to preserve the material evidence of his final, fatal endeavor, if that's what you want to do. I think it's probably safe to keep the house, if you want to do that, but…."

"After this evening?" she queried. "I don't think so. I've half a mind to sell it to Crisson, but he's such a terrible man."

"Money has no odor," I quoted, absent-mindedly, falling back into the slough of cliché.

"It's not a matter of money," she reminded me.

"I know that," I said. I reminded myself that I had just defended her against all the horrors in numerous universes, and had destroyed worlds in order to do it. Put like that, it didn't seem too terrible an ordeal, or too ridiculous an audacity, to say: "I love you." So I did.

She looked at me without surprise or alarm. "I know," she said, softly. "I've always known, and always felt terribly guilty about it."

"Oh," I said.

"I don't regret the choice I made, though," she said. "If I had to make it again, I'd do the same…and would doubtless have felt just as guilty, for just as long."

"Why feel guilty?" I said. "You made a choice, that's all."

"But it wasn't all, was it? As Crawford used to say, you can never do just one thing—what you do always has unintended side-effects. I knew when I made the choice that it hurt you. If I'd chosen differently, it would have hurt Crawford, and I'd have felt guilty about that too.

Sometimes, that's the way it is: whatever you do, someone gets hurt. I told myself at the time, to soothe my guilt, that you'd get over it, but I could see, as time went by, that you hadn't, so I felt worse. Even after the separation…I just felt guilty about that too."

"It wasn't your fault," I told her. "It was mine, for not being able to get over it."

"Don't do that," she said. "It doesn't diminish the guilt…it almost makes it worse. Sometimes, I almost wished that you'd hated me for it…but I couldn't do that either."

"Oh," I said. After a pause, I added: "I still love you."

"I know," she said, again.

"But whatever you decide to do, you really don't have to feel guilty any more," I said. "You never did, and if I'd known that you did, I'd have told you that you didn't have to. I understand. I always did understand. I will understand, if…."

She cut me off with a gesture. "I don't want to deceive you, David." she said. "I owe you that. You're my best friend. I'll marry you, if you want me to, but I don't want to do it under false pretences. I don't love you as much as I loved Crawford, and I never will. I wish I could, but I can't. Sometimes, that's the way it is. I can't explain it. I wish it were otherwise. I wish, now that Crawford's gone, that I could just flick a switch and transfer the feelings I had for him to you. God knows, you deserve that, at least, although you really deserve much better. I've exploited you, I fear, knowing how you felt. But I don't want to deceive you. It wouldn't be right."

"But you'll marry me if I want you to?" I said, just to check.

"If you want—but please think about it first. It might not be what you want, now that you know the truth. Perhaps I should have told you before, but there didn't seem to be any point, while Crawford was alive—although there might have been, because if I had told you, perhaps you could have found someone else, instead of just standing around in the wings of Crawford's life, forlorn. Even now, yesterday and today…I've been putting off telling you, like a coward, waiting for you to bring it up. I'm a terribly selfish person."

I opened my mouth.

"No," she said. "Not yet. You have to think about it first. Let me get all this legal stuff out of the way, settle things with the unholy three, one way or another, and then, if you still want something of me, I'll say yes to whatever you ask. Not just out of guilt, mind. I can't tell you that I'll ever feel for you what I felt or Crawford, but I do feel something. I think we might be happy together…perhaps happier than Crawford and

I were, however paradoxical that seems…but you need to be certain that you want me on those terms, because I don't want to pretend, or to lie to you."

There were tears in the corners of her eyes, but she blinked them away.

It was a shot in the heart for me, but it wasn't fatal. I understood. And anyway, I knew that the promise she'd made me was more than I deserved.

* * * *

The following day, Rachel sold the Tillinghast house and its contents to Robert Crisson, and went back to her house in the vicinity of New Bedford that evening. I went home, after arranging to meet her for dinner in a week's time.

I didn't feel defeated. How could I, given that I'd just defended an invasion attempt by aliens from the nth dimension single-handed, with a single gunshot? If I hadn't done it, who could? Nor Patterway, Crisson or Dove, that's for sure. I was a hero. I'd faced the ultimate horror—all of the ultimate horrors in series, in fact—and had come though…maybe not unscathed, but as James Patterway said, no one has survived an experience like that *unscathed.* I'd defied the odds, and I'd even defied the customary narrative logic of stories of that kind, in with the human characters almost always fall victim to the horrors.

No, I didn't feel defeated. I was even going to marry the only woman I'd ever loved in my life, and we were probably going to be happy, more or less. Not defeated at all. Victorious, in more ways that anyone with my conspicuous lack of talents and abilities has any right to expect.

Any yet….

And yet, my dutiful, mercilessly objective conscience persists in telling me, coldly, that my miserable, wretched, once-discontented life—even if it were multiplied a billion times—could not possibly counterbalance a trillionth of the damage that I did, in the pan of any reasonable scales of cosmic justice, when I fired that shot at the weather-vane on top of Crawford Tillinghast's house.

In the ultimate scheme of things, there has probably never been any evil greater than mine. There were horrors; I was threatened with death, or a worse fate; I had others to defend; my responsibility was absolutely clear.

But I feel guilty.

I know that I always will. Sometimes, that's the way it is.

But I did live through it, and I believe that I've conserved my sanity…or the better part of it…or, if not the better part, at least the remainder, the debris….

My companions lived through it too, and perhaps it was as well, for my sake, that they were there, to lend me their tacit support, even if they weren't much help, in practical terms.

When he had given the matter some thought, Patterway decided that, whatever Crisson said, no replica of Tillinghast's machine had ever put in an appearance, and that all the entities he had seen himself were mere hallucinations. Apparently, he has terrible migraines nowadays—I have that from Dove, who still keeps in touch with him, as he does with me.

Crisson didn't keep in touch with me or Dove, for the next few years, but he did with Patterway, so we continued to get news of him indirectly. Apparently, he eventually lost all interest in trying to reconstitute Tillinghast's machine. Even though he had seen the constitution of the improved model for himself, albeit briefly, before the shattered fragments of that replica were folded away into some fourth-dimensional pocket, or sewer, or bottomless abyss, he never made much headway with his own project. He searched high and low in Tillinghast's house for hidden papers, but never found any, and eventually sold it on, at a loss that would have been disconcerting for most people, but was only chicken-feed for him.

Dove continued occult his research, and continued to keep me fully informed. He still does but it really isn't very interesting: an endless series of anecdotes, which are bound seem lifeless to someone who had actually lived an experience of a similar sort, and certainly not the least of them.

Quite recently, Patterway resigned his professorship at Miskatonic and has gone on a long sea voyage—for the benefit of his health, he said. Crisson seems to have given up his attempts at invention, at least for the time being, and seems to be devoting himself go collecting art instead, although his tastes are far too *avant garde* for respectable New England, and he remains deeply unpopular in society. Lyman Dove, having written book after book summarizing the supposed secrets of the occult, seems to be making a certain amount of money out of them, and a certain notoriety.

Crisson told Patterway, before the latter set sail, that he intends to donate Tillinghast's papers to the library at Miskatonic, where they'll doubtless be filed away in some obscure corner. Whether anyone will ever consult them, I don't know. He also intends to give the university the shards of the machine as well, but without Patterway there to protect them, I suspect they'll eventually condemned as rubbish and thrown out.

The people to whom Crisson sold initially Tillinghast's house didn't live in it long, moving out because they felt uneasy there. It gained the reputation of being haunted, and still has it. It's derelict now. I've never been back there.

To judge by appearances, it's all over. The story even has a happy ending, because, in spite of Rachel's reservations, and the fact that she can't feel for me the passion she felt for Crawford Tillinghast, we are happy. I am, at least. Are Patterway, Crisson and Dove happy? I don't know, but I don't feel that it's particularly relevant to considering the end of the story to be happy. That only concerns Rachel and me. I hope she's happy too. I continue to be her loyal knight and shield against the threat of misfortune, although I haven't had much call to deploy my armaments since the crucial night of our relationship, when I destroyed universes.

That, alas, continues to be something of a worm in the fruit. I am happy, but I do still feel guilty. And I still suffer from occasional migraines, which force me to take laudanum to numb the pain, and when I take laudanum, I have dreams, or, rather, nightmares….and that reminds me that there's a sense it which it isn't really *over*, and never can be. The metamorphosis was permanent, you see. Nothing shows on the outside, but inside…my pineal body is quiet much of the time, allowing its sight to remain dormant, but when I feel a migraine coming on, I can see the floaters, and know what they are. And when I've taken the laudanum, I can see the dimensions beyond ours—not very far beyond, but still beyond. And I know that if I can see, then I can also be seen. What the consequences of that might be, I have no idea, but the fact remains.

One of the reasons why I maintained such an interest in the careers and actions of Patterway, Crisson and Dove is because I know that the brief exposure to the pure purple light that they endured was more than sufficient to plant metamorphic seeds in their brain: seeds that might have fallen on metaphorically stony ground, or might fail to germinate for any of the other multiple metaphorical reasons that might prevent seeds of enlightenment from germinating…but which might, over time, allow them to begin to see, and make them visible to other seers, elsewhere in the multiverse.

So what? Well, again, who can tell? Perhaps there will be no consequences at all.

I haven't said anything to Dove, or either of the others, or even to Rachel, about those seeds of metamorphosis. I'm quite content to allow everyone to stick to the story that what happened in the Tillinghast house that night was probably all a hallucination brought on by the purple glow, which was itself the result of some kind of residual miasma left over from her late husband's experiment. Rachel backs me up in that assertion, as a dutiful wife should.

Recently, I told Rachel that I was going to stop carrying a gun, and that in future I'll simply learn to live with my sense of insecurity as well my occasional migraines. She agrees wholeheartedly with that decision. I try not to take laudanum unless it's absolutely necessary, but she recognizes that it sometime is, even though the nightmares frighten her.

I don't like to frighten her, so I feel guilty about taking the laudanum, and not being able to stop having the migraines. Strangely enough, that guilt doesn't seem trivial, even though it's a very minor matter by comparison with the other guilt...but perhaps that's understandable, because the migraines, and the laudanum nightmares, bring the other guilt into its fullest, most furious flower. It's while I'm sick that I find myself asking how I can ever forgive myself, knowing what I have done, and knowing that I did it deliberately, having *taken aim*?

How can I even live with myself?

I don't think I could, if I didn't have Rachel, but I can't be sure—except when I have my migraines, and my pineal body allows my brain to see what it can nowadays see, under the right conditions. Then I'm sure, alas. According to my ophthalmologist, things can only get worse. One day, I'll probably go blind—and what will I see then? What will I be unable to avoid seeing, for lack of any possible distraction?

Monsters might come to devour me in the interim, I suppose—but that, perhaps strangely enough, always seems to be the least of my worries.

All in all, though, I have plenty for which to be thankful. The crisis really is over, and I really am happy—perhaps not completely, but what happiness ever is complete?

Into every life, as they say, a little rain must fall. You just have to make the most of the sunny periods, and the memory of having been, for once, a hero.

That heroism was not without its cost, but I just have to accept that, and keep polishing the memory so that the tarnish doesn't show.

Sometimes, that's the way it is.

www.ingramcontent.com/pod-product-compliance
Lightning Source LLC
Chambersburg PA
CBHW020653180626
46816CB00003B/1267